ISSUE 60: January 2023

Lezli Robyn, Editor
Lauren Rudin, Assistant Editor
Shahid Mahmud, Publisher

Published by Arc Manor/Phoenix Pick
P.O. Box 10339
Rockville, MD 20849-0339

Galaxy's Edge is published in January, March, May, July, September, and November.

All material is either copyright © 2023 by Arc Manor LLC, Rockville, MD, or copyright © by the respective authors as indicated within the magazine. All rights reserved.

This magazine (or any portion of it) may not be copied or reproduced, in whole or in part, by any means, electronic, mechanical or otherwise, without written permission from the publisher, except by a reviewer who may quote brief passages in a review.

Please check our website for submission guidelines.

ISBN: 978-1-64973-133-3

SUBSCRIPTION INFORMATION:
Paper and digital subscriptions are available (including via Amazon.com) . Please visit our home page: www.GalaxysEdge.com

ADVERTISING:
Advertising is available in all editions of the magazine. Please contact advert@GalaxysEdge.com.

FOREIGN LANGUAGE RIGHTS:
Please refer all inquiries pertaining to foreign language rights to Shahid Mahmud, Arc Manor, P.O. Box 10339, Rockville, MD 20849-0339. Tel: 1-240-645-2214. Fax 1-310-388-8440. Email admin@ArcManor.com.

CONTENTS

EDITOR'S NOTE by Lezli Robyn — 3

MOTHER'S LOVE, FATHER'S PLACE by Oghenechovwe Donald Ekpeki — 4

THE LAST MAN by Eric Leif Davin — 10

TOURING by Gardner Dozois, Jack Dann, and Michael Swanwick — 15

CAIN AND ABEL by Yefim Zozulya, translated by Alex Shvartsman — 25

THE GARDENER OF CERES by Marc A. Criley — 29

OLD MACDONALD HAD A FARM by Mike Resnick — 35

LEAP OF FAITH by Alan Smale — 43

THE LAMENT CONFIGURATION by Alicia Cay — 58

GALAXY'S EDGE INTERVIEWS NISI SHAWL by Jean Marie Ward — 64

RECOMMENDED BOOKS by Richard Chwedyk — 69

TURNING POINTS *(column)* by Alan Smale — 74

LONGHAND *(column)* by L. Penelope — 77

THE REFLECTION ON MOUNT VITAKI *(Serialization, Part II)* by Kristine Kathryn Rusch — 79

May 2023

EDITOR'S NOTE

by Lezli Robyn

With a brand New Year starting, so begins a new season for the magazine. The 60th issue of Galaxy's Edge marks several significant milestones. We've printed six issues per year for an entire decade, publishing an incredible 646 pieces of flash fiction, short stories, novelettes and novellas! Along with novel serializations, interviews, and regular columns, our magazine has published the first story sales of new authors in nearly every issue, staying true to Mike Resnick's intention for *Galaxy's Edge* to shine a spotlight on emerging writers in science fiction and fantasy.

With Mike Resnick at the editing helm for the first seven years of the magazine, he discovered and published many new Writer Children, as well as buying stories from Big Names in this field, until his passing in 2020. When I took over, I knew I had very big shoes to fill, and my last three years editing the magazine has been a highlight of my career. During that time, we created an online submissions system, dramatically increasing our international submissions, and have experienced the pleasure of publishing fiction by authors that became finalists or winners of major awards in the field (the Aurora, British Fantasy, BSFA, Hugo, Nebula, and Nommo Awards!).

But just as the publishing market is evolving, so are we. The magazine is published by Arc Manor, a company that has gone through significant expansion over the last two years, and these changes offer us some new and exciting opportunities.

Issue 62 will be last installment of *Galaxy's Edge* in the format it's currently published. Then the magazine will be converted into a bi-annual anthology book series, with the first volume being published at the end of 2023! Not only will we continue to bring you the fiction our readers have grown to love so much, but this new format will make it easier to get into brick-and-mortar bookstores through a full-service distributor. It will also allow us to raise the rates we pay our authors as well as give us greater flexibility to buy more novelettes and novellas, which has been restricted by the current format.

As the editor for the new *Galaxy's Edge* anthology series, I cannot wait to spotlight new authors alongside some of the biggest names in the field. And all while increasing our audience base. The coming year is going to be an exciting one for us, and we cannot wait to share more updates with our authors and readers!

But first, let me tell you more about this milestone issue. In Alicia Cay's short story, "The Lament Configuration," we find out how parting with something sentimental during the heartache of grief can lead to a return gift of healing much more profound. The magic and heart Alicia infuses into her words are just so incredibly beautiful; this story's end notes brought this editor to tears.

In Eric Leif Davin's "The Last Man," we are given a disturbing glimpse of human relations in a post-apocalyptic world, and in "The Gardner of Ceres" by Marc A. Criley, we are shown another example of what one woman would do to save the love of her life. Marc's story is filled with such rich and beautiful world-building, I really wish for his future to come true—I would definitely board a colonization ship to move to his version of Ceres!

Alex Shvartsman deftly translates Yefim Zozulya's fable, "Cain and Abel," which for some readers will seem like a version of history, and for others pure fantasy, depending on your belief system. We round out the fiction in this issue with another incredible piece by Oghenechovwe Donald Ekpeki that will stop you in your tracks with its profound message, the final part in Kristine Kathryn Rusch's serialization, and classic reprints by Mike Resnick, our regular columnist Alan Smale, and collaborators Gardner Dozois, Jack Dann, and Michael Swanwick.

Along with our regular columns by L. Penelope and Alan Smale, and a new list of Recommended Books by Richard Chwedyk, Jean Marie Ward interviews Nisi Shawl! As a lover of everything mermaid, their conversation is a pure delight and the perfect addition to this issue.

We hope our readers had a wonderful holiday season, and a successful start to the New Year. We look forward to including you on our new publishing journey throughout 2023! As always, happy reading! I can't wait to see what this new season gifts us.

Oghenechovwe Donald Ekpeki is an African speculative fiction writer, editor & publisher in Nigeria. He has won the Nommo award twice, and Otherwise and British Fantasy awards. His novelette "O$_2$ Arena" won the Nebula award, and was a Hugo award finalist, making him the first African to be a Nebula best novelette winner and Hugo best novelette finalist. The thought-provoking piece was also a finalist for British Science Fiction, British Fantasy and Nommo awards. He edits The Year's Best African Speculative Fiction *anthology series, and for Volume One he was the first African Hugo award finalist for Best Editor. He's also the first BIPOC to be a Hugo award finalist in fiction* and *editing categories in the same year, and* The Year's Best African Speculative Fiction Volume One *anthology he edited and published was also British Fantasy finalist and a World Fantasy award winner.*

MOTHER'S LOVE, FATHER'S PLACE

by Oghenechovwe Donald Ekpeki

Bassey walked bare-chested into his wife's hut, where she was being attended by the midwife and her two younger apprentices. His sweaty, gleaming muscles reflected the faint light cast by the candles in the hut. He exchanged a look with his wife, then turned to the midwife.

"May I have a moment with my wife?"

"Her time is done and she may begin to push any moment from now."

"I'll be brief," he said with suppressed impatience.

The midwife glanced at Ofonime, who every now and then mopped the sweat on her brow with the edge of her wrapper. Ofonime nodded at the midwife, who motioned to her apprentices, and the trio left the hut for husband and wife.

Bassey grumbled at the departing women. "Warriors get less and less respect these days. See what regard I get as a Captain! These missionaries of a foreign god and their acolytes are doing a great harm to our people with their gospel of peace and equality…"

"Same missionaries advocate for the lives of twins, something that you may be interested in." She said this with a pointed look.

He hesitated, then said, "Just because they seek what *may* be to my advantage, doesn't make them my friends. One thing I have learned is, the assumption that the enemy of my enemy is my friend … does not guarantee survival. It will soon leave our entire way of life eroded and our land sacked and looted."

"But it will get you through a long night of battle will it not?"

He huffed at this. "And what would you know of battles and long nights?" he mused, amusement heavy in his tone.

"Am I not about to face one now my husband? A battle and a long night?"

He stopped as his eyes rested on the frightened and anxious look on his wife's face. He stared at her askance. But in place of an answer, she raised two fingers at him.

"Are you sure?" he asked, hoping to be contradicted.

"I have no doubts," she said. "I have suspected it for a while. Now I am certain."

He was silent a moment, then he started, "That means we have to—to—"

"Eliminate one of them?" she interrupted him with a choked sob.

He nodded and laid a hand on her shoulder. "We may yet cut our losses," he said. "I shall pour some money into the mid-wife's pocket to dispose of one but leave us with the other. That way, we can circumvent the abomination and attendant consequences."

"No, no, no," Ofonime protested, shaking her head vigorously. "I shall not live to see any of them eliminated."

"The second of the twins is a child of a spirit union. It will bring nothing but destruction to us. Would you rather we be disgraced and destroyed than eliminate the abomination?"

She brought her distraught eyes to his face, looking deeply hurt. "You do believe it then, that I was unfaithful to you with a spirit? I, who has never had another man apart from you—took a spirit to my bed?"

"I don't doubt you," Bassey said. "But even then, you know the customs. Had we left for the Ekoi when you told me … But as a warrior and captain and member of the Ekpe fraternity, my place is here, a place of honour, with my children and family. We have everything to lose by leaving."

"No, my husband," Eso said sadly. "*you* have everything to lose. Your children, your family, your place." She spat that last out. "*None* of it mine, at least that I would keep by allowing the killing of my child. I have given you my body. But I will not allow you to bribe the midwife to deliver and dispose of one of my children as you and your other fraternity members do."

Bassey stared at his wife, unable to deny her words.

"Do you think that we women don't talk amongst ourselves? We know this is what you do. But you'll not succeed in my case. I will deliver both my babies."

Bassey shook his head. "The two children will be taken from us, put in a pot and left in the evil forest to die. You will be exiled at best, or killed."

"I will not sanction the killing of one of my children to escape the fate decreed by men of old Calabar. I will be exiled or die with my children if I have to."

He was quiet a moment, considering the resolve in her voice. She had never argued with him before, but it seemed her submission had her limits. Nor did it seem that she was simply overcome with the high of panicked hysteria that accompanied birth. Bassey was momentarily angry—why would she disobey him? Right now, right at this time? But then, he was unsure what he would do in her place. His next words carried more admiration than censure.

"Your love for your children is great, even if it will doom us all. Will you hold off delivery for as long as you can? I want to consult with Archibong and see what the spirits have to say."

"I will hold off delivery as much as I can. I love you, but once my children come, I owe them the duty of protection. I'll not sanction the death of any of them, even for you. If you do not value their lives, do not return to us."

Bassey turned to leave. As he stepped out of the hut, the head midwife confronted him.

"Has the arrangement been made, Captain?"

"I haven't decided."

"Decide fast, for the hour is almost upon us." She spat. "It is bad enough for me to be part of bringing your cursed offspring to life, but I won't do it for free."

Bassey glared at her but kept his cool. "Do nothing foolish until I return."

✧

Bassey walked into the house of Archibong, the priest of Ekpe fraternity.

"My friend," Bassey saluted. "I need your services."

Archibong smiled and led him to a special alcove in his house, dropping the curtains behind them. He sat on the floor, cross-legged. Bassey sat facing him. The room was accoutered like a shrine. Lanterns and candles dotted the place, but their light only served to deepen the shadows it could not touch. The darkness clung to the walls and the sacred objects in the room. Behind them was a bowl of water from which rose steam, though there was no fire lit under it. The grotesque features of masks and the regalia of masquerades hanging on the walls leered at them. Archibong himself had one of his eyes rounded with white chalk and his neck and hands were loaded with cowry necklaces and hand beads.

"You were expecting me?" Bassey asked.

Archibong smiled. "Far is the sight that needs no eye to see, my friend. I see things before they manifest, be they inside a man's vestments or a woman's belly. But I suspect your affairs are far from hidden even to mundane eyes."

"They are not?" Bassey asked with glittering eyes.

"Of course. Being favoured by King Eyo makes you interesting to watch. And anyone with eyes knows which omens to seek to find out if a woman will bear twins."

Bassey snorted. "They may speculate and peddle rumours, but they have no proof."

"And how long before the proof is born and their rumours justified? You will do well to be swift in dispatching the cursed one. Eyes are on you. Your brother warrior and rival, Offiong, has been spying on you and his blood is hot to displace you as the Obong Ebong title holder."

Bassey dismissed the threat with a wave of the hand. "Longer may he wait for the office. He is a toothless dog and lacks the charisma that moves men to proper action. He lacks the mettle to carry out his schemes. I do not worry about him. I worry about the fate and destiny of both my unborn children. That is why I'm here." Moreover, King Eyo's favour was won by more than such selfish ambitions.

The king had some strange notions, but good things came to those who could carry them out.

Archibong sighed with raised eyebrows. He hadn't missed Bassey's claiming of the children. "I hope you know what you are doing, old friend. And I hope you are right about your old rival."

The priest pulled at one of the necklaces on his neck and it cut, spilling its beads on the floor. Archibong's eyes watched the spiritual ordering of the beads as they danced and became still. He read the cowries on the floor quietly for a moment. Bassey opened his mouth, about to demand what tidings the spirits bore for him, but Archibong's raised finger forestalled him.

"They wish to speak to you."

"Who?" Bassey said in alarm.

"Your children wish to speak to you."

Bassey was about to query the priest when the lights went out and the room was plunged into pitch blackness. Then a faint light intruded. Bassey squinted at what appeared to be a misty dawn.

He was in a glade filled with sunshine and laughter and running water. Children of varying ages played around him, carefree and light-footed. He turned about and saw a figure walking towards him. It was a sturdy young man, with a firm jaw and broad shoulders. Bassey was struck by the familiarity of the face: it was a reflection of his younger self.

"Father," the younger man said, walking towards Bassey with a smile. "I bear the tidings of the spirits."

Bassey opened his mouth to speak, but the words stuck in his throat.

"I am our spokesperson. In the forward flow of time, you accepted us both, though you yet have not decided. I come as the one you have accepted for the present."

Just beyond the clearing, a woman peeked out from behind a tree. She bore a great resemblance to the young man approaching Bassey, and as their eyes met, she broke into a smile. It was an echo of Ofonime's.

Bassey turned back to solemnly regard the apparition which looked so much like himself. "What must I do, my son? What do the spirits bid me do? Do I give up the soul of the many for the one I have not chosen?" Could he give up her soul, now, having seen her?

"You have chosen, my father," the apparition said, "just as you have been chosen. In choosing us both, you chose the many unborn twins that will be cast away in misguided sacrifice. In saving one, you will save the many. This is what the spirits bid deliver to you."

The other apparition came forward and laid her hand on Bassey's chest as he tried to speak. The spirit's hand was a warm, testament to the reality of this place's existence, and this child's future. Bassey knew his son's spirit spoke true. He could no more deny choosing her than he could deny the beating of his heart.

"Go now, my father. Save us and raise us, that we may raise you."

Bassey raised his arms to embrace his children, but their forms faded into him, enveloping him in darkness. His eyes opened to the yellow flames of Archibong's room.

"Welcome back, my friend. Have you received your message?"

Bassey nodded. "I know what I must do."

Archibong nodded in understanding. Both men stood up and hugged. Archibong held Bassey at arm's length, silently taking him in. They both knew this was farewell.

✧

In the birthing house, the head midwife placed the second twin on Ofonime's breast, having cut the umbilical cord and cleaned it. Her disgust was evident on her face. She had held the baby at arm's length while handling it. The new mother of the twins glowed with relief despite the impending doom she anticipated. She held the babies protectively, announcing without words her willingness to die for them if need be, in defiance of the custom that declared them taboo.

She saw the disgust on the midwife's face and asked, "If you hate my children so, why did you deliver them?"

The midwife's eyes bulged, unwilling to believe that she was being questioned by one consigned to destruction. "Your children might be spawn of evil, but I do my duty as a midwife. I leave the men to purge the evils you have brought to the land. I shall send for them immediately." So saying, she beckoned to one of her apprentices.

Ofonime pleaded with the midwife. "Please Uwemedimoh," Ofonime called her by name, hoping to invoke mercy through familiarity. "You know us. You came for my sister's marriage ceremony and delivered her three children. We are not strangers, for you to be so heartless to me. At least let their father see them first."

The midwife's brows were full of scorn. "Because I brought your cursed offspring into life does not mean I shall not do my duty of alerting the land to the curse you have brought out of your belly." She spat on the bed at Ofonime, her spittle just narrowly missing her.

Ofonime looked at her, her eyes hardening. "You didn't deliver them out of duty. You delivered them because you are too cowardly to actualise your hate yourself. You delivered them out of weakness, and greed." Ofonime held her babies closer.

The midwife's eyes fluttered in her skull, glittering doorways of evil that offered a glimpse to a dark realm beyond. Her fingers were curled like eagle's talons, and she glared at Ofonime and her babies as if contemplating strangling them in her grip, a grip slick with wickedness. She even took a step forward but snapped out of it at the sudden wailing of one of the babies.

The midwife turned to the apprentice. "Run to the guards and the council and inform them of the atrocity that has happened here."

But the girl had hardly left the room when she stumbled back in, shoved back by Bassey. The midwife shouted at the girl to go get the guards. She took one look at Bassey's imposing, bulky figure dwarfing the door, and stepped further back. The midwife stepped forward in anger and Bassey's fist caught her by the throat, lifting her easily off the ground. She struggled and gasped for breath, her face turning purple as she asphyxiated. The midwife's frightened apprentices stumbled to and fro. But for Ofonime's voice calling repeatedly to Bassey, he might have killed the midwife.

There was no anger in Bassey's face, only curiosity and determination. He let go of her and she crumpled to the floor in an unceremonious heap.

Ofonime laid the babies down and struggled to stand. Bassey rushed to assist her but froze at the sight of the babies. They were no longer apparitions in the spirit world, but now flesh and blood, wailing with loud voices as if to impress into his ears that they lived.

"You would have killed her," Ofonime said.

"She would have killed my children and wife."

"She is not the problem. Our ways are. Killing her won't kill the problem."

"She is part of the problem and killing her will kill a part of the problem." Bassey didn't know why he hadn't thought about it before. It all seemed so simple now.

Ofonime shook her head. "You are a great warrior, but you are not famous for cleverness." She bent and pulled a bunch of wrappers from under the bed, throwing them at the girls helping the midwife massage her throat. "Tie her up," she instructed them.

The girls sat staring, motionless.

"Now!" Bassey barked. And they rushed to comply with his order. He turned to Ofonime. The babies were now quiet, asleep. He cupped her cheeks. "I have decided. Both my children must live. They have a great destiny."

Ofonime held his hand on her cheek, breathing deeply.

Bassey continued. "But we must leave, now."

Ofonime glanced at the sleeping babies in concern.

"They will be fine," he said. He gave no further explanation. Relating to her his vision of the grown twins would only create more questions and delays, and there would be time later to tell Ofonime about their tall son, their beautiful daughter.

She moved to wrap them more securely.

Bassey turned to the girls, who had tied up the midwife securely. "You will stay here and guard her. You will not leave this hut till the light of dawn dots the horizon. If you do, I will find you and kill you. Do you understand me?"

They nodded in fright. Bassey and his wife and newborns slipped out of the hut.

As they stepped out, they were confronted by the figure of Ukeme, Bassey's second wife. The trio froze, staring at each other without speaking. Bassey gripped his slipping spear tighter, as his palm was slick with sweat.

Ukeme spoke first, her eyes narrowing "I knew what you were up to. I just wanted to see with my own eyes, you abandoning us to abscond with her!" she said this, with a glare at Ofonime, who dropped her eyes. "We were always nice to you, I and mama Nkeme. Now you repay us by stealing our husband?"

Bassey sighed, taking her hand and pulling her aside. "I am a warrior, not an object. She's not stealing me. She's trying to live, with her children. And she can't without me. Unlike you."

Ukeme folded her arms, not placated. "You have been a good father thus far. A good father and husband. Now you abandon your other wives and children and place here." She whistled and a young lad came forward from the shadows where he had been standing. A boy of about five years.

The boy walked up to Bassey, then seeing it was his father, rushed to embrace him. Bassey bent to hug him.

"Your youngest. He dotes on you. Wants to be a warrior like you when he grows. You would leave him without even a goodbye?"

Bassey held the boy back, at arm's length. Though his heart hurt, he was grateful for this chance to speak to his child. In a better world, he would not have to choose between any of his children. "My son, part of being a warrior is knowing the right and most important battles to fight. A mother's place is to love her children with her life, and a father's place is to protect the mother. Someday when you grow up, if I have done my job half as well as your mother says, you will understand this. Okay?"

The boy nodded solemnly, trusting in his father's wisdom, and he went to his mother who had beckoned to him.

Bassey looked at his second wife and formerly youngest son. "You will both be fine. He has his mother. And you have the rest of the town."

Ukeme was silent for a while, then she nodded. "Go be a good father, my husband. And husband," she added, with a side glance at Ofonime. She nodded at Ofonime, who smiled gratefully. "Farewell. I never saw you tonight." Having said that, she took her son's hand and faded into the night. Bassey and Ofonime with their twin babies did the same.

☼

They made their way out of town with Ofonime carrying the two children, swaddled safely in blankets, and shuffling after Bassey who led the way with a spear clutched in his hand. He peered in every direction.

"Perhaps you could let go of the spear and hold one of your children," she said.

"We are not past the danger yet," he rebuked gently, his voice soft in the night. "My enemies shadow me and I must be on alert. I told you my rival Offiong will seek me and try to disgrace me for my place of honour with the king and in the Ekpe confraternity. It is not enough for me to just leave." He would offer, even though he was unused to carrying children long distances. They would travel faster with a baby apiece, but if they were ambushed, he did not want to chance being off-balance and thus put them all in danger.

"Men and their rivalry. If only you left me and my children out of it," she grumbled.

"Be quiet, woman. Haven't I given up enough? My place, for you and your children and a life of exile?"

"How gracious of you," she muttered, ensuring he did not hear her.

Bassey continued talking. "A boat is waiting for us by the river to take us to the Ekoi where twins are celebrated."

Ofonime was silent. Her husband seemed to have had it all worked out, except that he had not considered the plight of carrying newborns just hours after a rigorous labour.

Bassey stopped suddenly. She looked askance at him, distraught.

"Keep going," he said. "When you get to the river, you will find someone to paddle the boat and bear you away, if I don't join you on time." He forestalled her protests with a kiss. "You have done your part. Let me do mine." He shoved her gently.

She trotted away, looking back at him as she went. He didn't look back. He stood facing the other direction as the sound of footsteps became clearer. A group of men emerged from the night, spat out of the shadows by the envy of Offiong. He and about a dozen men approached. They stopped when they saw Bassey waiting with his spear extended in a stance of ready combat.

They approached cautiously. Bassey motioned towards the direction they just came from and they looked up at the sky to see a plume of smoke rising from the direction of the palace.

Offiong stepped forward. "What have you done, traitor?"

"You didn't think I wouldn't cover my escape, did you? I started a fire at the palace before I left. And I have people waiting to ambush and kill the king in the chaos. He will die, along with your hopes and wishes for power. Perhaps the new king won't be so disposed to favour the warriors that failed the prior one."

Offiong spluttered in anger. "You're mad, you traitor!" He motioned to his men. "Rush to the palace to warn the king of an ambush. I will kill this traitor myself and drag his wife back to burn with his cursed spawn."

The men started to rush back the way they came, as Offiong unslung his cutlass.

Bassey's eyes glittered. "I might have merely maimed you and let you live if you had left my wife and children out of it."

Offiong rushed forward with a snarl and slashed at Bassey, who sidestepped his swing smoothly and swept him off his feet with the haft of the spear. In one smooth motion, he planted the sharp end into Offiong's gut as he fell, pinning him to the earth. Offiong groaned and struggled. Bassey plunged the spear further through Offiong and into the soft earth.

"Stay on the ground where you belong, vile serpent. You will be a long time dying."

Offiong was grinning even in his pain. Blood burbled off his lips as he struggled to talk. "I have sent men to the boats. Your escape is cut off. I win…"

Bassey turned back in shock. He pulled the spear from Offiong's gut and ran after his wife. Offiong's wheezing laughter combined with his blubber and tears of pain chased Bassey onward.

☼

Bassey and Ofonime walked on in the night. He had discarded his spear now and carried one of the twins while his wife carried the other.

"Offiong might as well have killed us rather than simply cut off our escape," Ofonime said. "We are doomed to be inevitably found and worse would befall us."

"We shall triumph," Bassey said simply.

"How? Where do we go now?"

"The forest," he answered.

"What?" she exclaimed. "The evil forest? The same forest where monsters and evil spirits devour twins left there to die by the people of the land?"

"May I have peace, woman," Bassey said wearily. "There is a path through the forest. Through it we can make our way to the Ekoi."

"If we don't all die there," Ofonime grumbled. "I did not leave Old Calabar only to come here and die."

As they plunged into the forest, Ofonime trembled at the thought of the numerous twins who had been brought here to die and whose souls were left here to languish. The forest grew less dark, and eventually the leaves glimmered with dawn's twilight. But it was too soon for dawn.

She adjusted her arms to hold up her baby, and instead found they both held bundles of cloths where they each had held a child. She was about to cry out to Bassey, wondering if she was hallucinating from her tiredness, when she saw him grin.

"Look! Our children are there."

Where he pointed, two figures ran towards them, their arms wide open with welcome.

☼

King Eyo stood in front of the smoking ruins of his palace. He couldn't quite believe Bassey had really done what he said he would do, but the evidence was right in front of him. Not only had his top warrior followed through on the pretense of betrayal, he had opened the opportunity for a reform, as promised.

"We will find the traitor, your majesty," the king's adviser said.

"No!" the king barked. "Haven't you shed blood enough? Let him be. What has happened was bound to happen. Unless we change our way, I foresee more woes to come."

"But it is our custom," protested the advisor. "Twins have always been taboo. It is the law that they be put to death and Bassey committed…"

The king raised his finger and his adviser stopped talking.

"Send for the chiefs," King Eyo said. "I have some strong words to pass to all and sundry under my domain. A culture which has outlived its use is dispatched with a bad year."

Copyright © 2022 by Oghenechovwe Donald Ekpeki.
First appeared in Don't Touch That:
An Anthology of Parenthood in SFF.

This is Eric Leif Davin's eighth story in Galaxy's Edge. *Two of his previous stories were chosen for* The Year's Best Military & Adventure SF *anthologies from Baen Books, edited by David Afsharrirad. Eric is also the author of* Pioneers of Wonder: Conversations With the Founders of Science Fiction, *from Prometheus Books, and* Partners in Wonder: Women and the Birth of Science Fiction, 1926-1965, *from Lexington Books.*

THE LAST MAN

by Eric Leif Davin

I pushed the shopping cart down the aisle, filling it with canned goods from the grocery store shelves. The cart was balky; rusty wheels made the cart harder to push, the more I loaded it up. But, I was in no rush—there was nowhere I had to be.

I concentrated on canned goods. Rats had eaten holes in most of the boxed foods. The contents spilled out and poured over the shelves and into piles on the floor. If we became desperate enough, we could start scooping that up, but there was no need to, just yet. Meanwhile, better to avoid anything the rats ate. They may be carrying the Virus.

We never knew what the Virus was. There was always some new disease slipping over from the animal kingdom into the human population: AIDS, Ebola, Zika, Coronavirus, whatever. We'd always been able to deal with them, eventually. Not so with the latest one. It came out of nowhere and spread across the globe, leaping from continent to continent with the speed of the jet airliners that probably carried it to the far corners of the earth. It was far more lethal than any previous new disease. It wiped out entire populations within months, weeks, even days. There was no way to contain it, no time to even name it. It was just the Virus.

Some of us, however, had some kind of natural immunity. We lived, while everyone else died. Our hearts broke, while all the others stopped beating. Now we just survived as best we could amid the detritus of vanished humanity.

I'd piled the cart high with my cans. I had cans of veggies, soups, beef stew, fruit. I tried to give us a balanced diet. The labels had fallen off some of the cans, their glue loosening over time. We saved those cans for Sunday night dinners, so we could have a surprise when we opened them—a little dinner delight to add a little bit of "different" to an otherwise monotonous post-apocalyptic existence. It didn't matter what the cans contained; we ate most anything, except beets. We'd have to really run low on food before we'd eat beets. But, that wasn't going to happen soon. There were plenty of other grocery stores where I could shop after I stripped this one bare.

Then I saw him.

Ahead of me, looming large at the end of the aisle was a man. In one hand he had a red plastic shopping basket, filled with cans and some boxes that he'd taken from the stack by the entrance. In his other hand he carried some kind of assault rifle with a banana clip. He was staring at me wide-eyed, in shocked silence. I stared back, not moving, not saying a word, though my heart was suddenly pounding.

Then I was gone, bolting back the way I'd come. I reached the end of the aisle and skidded around it. He was between the front entrance and me, so I headed for the back loading dock.

As soon as I started to run, he dropped his food basket and came charging down the aisle after me. He also skidded around the end of the aisle. "Wait! Don't run!" he yelled. "I won't hurt you!" I glanced back and saw he still had the rifle, so I poured on the speed. I wasn't taking any chances.

I slammed through the double doors in the rear of the store and ran for the curtain of plastic strips hanging at the exit to the loading dock. He was right behind me. I brushed the strips aside, reached the edge of the dock, and jumped. He did the same.

I hit the asphalt and rolled, but before I could be up and running, he landed on top of me, his assault rifle clattering to the side. I twisted and tried to throw him off, but his big male bulk weighed me down. He straddled my waist and grabbed my arms, forcing me onto my back. He pinned my arms to the pavement and sat on me as I struggled and grunted. His face, bearded and grimy, hovered over me, inches from mine. "I'm not going to hurt you," he kept saying. "I'm not going to hurt you." His stinking breath choked me; he clearly had not been availing himself of the many tubes of toothpaste still in abundance on store shelves.

I realized I wasn't going anywhere, so I stopped struggling and stared up at his filthy face. He lowered his voice and kept repeating, "I'm not going to hurt you," in what he hoped was a soothing tone. I guess it was. Though my heart was still hammering against my ribs, my ragged breath slowed and I began to calm down. I stared in silence up into his eyes, still wide in wonder, and waited for his next move.

"You're a woman," he said, as if in awe.

"No shit, Sherlock."

"What are you doing here?"

"Shopping. Isn't that what women do?"

"No, I mean, *here*." He nodded around us. "I thought I was the last man alive."

"You might be. I haven't seen any others lately."

"I mean…I thought I was the last *person* alive." Then he stared down at me piercingly. "Are you alone?"

I stared back and said nothing.

"Look, you don't have to be afraid of me. I'm not going to hurt you. I'm sorry if I scared you back there. I was just as surprised to see you, as you were to see me. I haven't seen anyone else in…*years*."

"If you're not going to hurt me, then get off me."

"Okay, just please don't run away."

I grunted. Slowly, he rose and stood beside me. I sat up, turned to get to my knees…then I was up and running, like a sprinter bursting out of the blocks.

And I went down just as fast, with the big man wrapped around my ankles. I tried to kick myself free, kick him in his face, but he held on and wrestled himself up my body. He forced me over onto my belly and pulled my arms behind me. Then he lashed my hands together with a short length of rope he pulled from his belt. "I'm sorry to do this, but I guess I have to…for now."

He sat on my butt and neither of us said a word as my breath puffed up tiny wisps of dirt from the asphalt beneath my face. I relaxed and my forehead touched the pavement. I closed my eyes and waited for what would happen next. If he tried to rape me, I'd have a chance to kick him in the balls and make another run for it.

Finally, he spoke. "You had a lot of cans in that cart back there. Taking it home for somebody?"

I said nothing, my breath continuing to puff up pavement dust.

"Is there a community? A group? I can be a valuable addition."

I said nothing.

"Look, I told you, I'm not going to hurt you. I'm not going to rape you. I just don't want you to run away."

"Then let me up and untie me."

"I'll let you up, but I won't untie you. And I'm going to hold on to this end of the rope so you can't run away."

He got up off my butt and stood beside me, the rope firmly in his fist, as I struggled to my knees. Then I paused, kneeling, with my hands tied behind me, staring at the dust and thinking about what I should do next. He had me and it seemed I needed some help.

"My name's Andy," he said. "What's yours?"

"Valerie."

"So, Valerie, who were you taking all the food home for?"

I sighed. "For Lucy."

"So, there are two of you?"

"Yeah. There are two of us."

I glanced up at him. A big shit-eating grin spread slowly across his face. "Well, well," he said. "From famine to feast."

I called out for Lucy as we approached the house, an enormous McMansion in what had been an upscale suburban neighborhood before the Virus emptied it. There was no longer any electricity. Nor was there running water, but one reason we'd picked this particular McMansion was because there was a stream in the small grove of woods behind it and that stream now ran pure and unpolluted. Deer, rabbits, and raccoons came down to drink from it. Lately, even small fish had begun to appear in it. Nature was reclaiming the human world. So, we had water.

When we needed food, we shopped at the local shopping mall, within walking distance. Which is where I'd run into Andy, now walking behind me, his backpack stuffed with my canned goods, the end of the rope that tied my hands in his left fist, his assault rifle held warily in his right.

Lucy popped into view at an open upper window, smiling and waving. Both the smile and the wave froze when she saw us, and she dropped from sight.

"Does she have a gun?"

"We don't have any guns. We don't need'em."

"Wish I could believe you."

When we reached the front door Andy reached for the knob and turned it. The door was unlocked, of course, and it swung open easily at his touch. He pushed me inside and then followed slowly. I walked into my home. Light flooded in from the tall narrow windows that fronted the spacious entrance lobby of the McMansion.

"Where is she?" Andy glanced nervously around the entrance and up at the two-story high cathedral ceiling. Second floor balconies ringed the entrance. It was ideal for an ambush. If you had a gun.

"I have no idea."

"Anything happens, you'll get it first."

"Nothing will happen." Then I raised my voice. "Lucy! This is Andy! He says he won't hurt us!"

"Then why does he have a gun?" Lucy called back from somewhere in the caverns of our home. "Why are your hands tied?"

I looked at Andy. "Good questions. Why are my hands still tied? And why are you waving that gun? I *told* you, we don't have any guns."

"Okay, Lucy," Andy yelled. "I'm going to untie Valerie. You come on out and show me you don't have a gun and I'll lower my gun. I don't mean you any harm. I just want to be safe."

Andy untied my hands with his left hand while still holding his assault rifle at the ready with his right. As he did so, he glanced quickly from the knots he was untying to the balconies and side rooms off the lobby and then back again to the knots. As the rope fell free, he grabbed the hair at the back of my head to hold me in place.

"OK, I've untied Valerie. Come on out. I won't hurt you."

Lucy half-emerged from the shadows of a side room and lingered at the doorway, ready to flee in an instant. Even in the shadows her blonde mane seemed to glow in the sunlight streaming in from the tall narrow windows in the lobby and, even as Andy held my own hair in one clenched fist and his assault rife in the other, I marveled at how beautiful she was.

Andy smiled at her. "See," he said, lowering his rifle. "I just want to be friends."

He released my hair and Lucy and I ran to each other. We embraced fiercely and I kissed her on the neck as I held her tight to me.

"I was so afraid for you," Lucy gasped.

"No reason to be afraid. I'm okay. It's all going to be fine."

Andy smiled at the two of us, hugging in the light of our cathedral lobby. "Of course it is," he said. "We're going to be just one big happy family."

☼

That evening Lucy fixed the three of us a nice warm meal. Andy had lugged home several cans of the beef stew that I'd loaded into my cart. We poured them all together into the big cast iron pot we had suspended over our backyard fireplace. With the thicket of woods so close by, we had all the firewood we needed. The aroma from the bubbling stew wafted into the open back door and filled the kitchen with its luscious scent.

"Long time since I've had a home cooked meal by a pretty woman," Andy said.

Lucy was cutting up homegrown carrots and onions from our garden to add to the stew. She ignored him. I was sitting at the kitchen table with Andy, sipping at my coffee.

"So, Andy, what are your plans?"

Andy swallowed a mouthful of his own coffee and placed the mug on the table. His assault rifle leaned against his thigh. He smiled at me. When he did so, his matted beard parted enough to reveal cratered teeth. I guess that was why his breath stank so much when he had me on the ground.

"Don't you worry, Valerie, my wandering days are over. I've found my piece of paradise and I'm staying right here with the two of you."

"This is our home."

"And now it's *my* home, too." He looked between the both of us, considering. "Surely you ladies have missed the company of a man, after all these lonely years. We could fill the house with our children."

Lucy chopped the carrots a bit louder at that, the knife slicing through and banging into the wooden cutting board beneath. She glanced over at Andy. "I think not."

He didn't hear her—or was unwilling to listen. "We'll start the human race all over and I'll be Adam with my two Eves!" He threw back his head and laughed loudly at that. "God! How lucky can a man be?"

My teeth clenched. "Andy, Lucy and I don't *want* to have any children. We're happy just the way we are."

Andy roared again with laughter. "Of *course* you want children! *All* women want children! It's part of your nature."

"Well, it's not part of *our* nature."

Andy stopped laughing and looked closely at me. Then he looked over at Lucy, now chopping the onions, her blonde hair falling forward to conceal her face. "Oh, I get it." He smiled broadly, another of his fantasies unlocked. "You two have been making it with each other! It's understandable. Two women, all alone with each other, no man around. It's the women-behind-bars thing. I understand. But *Andy's* here now! I can satisfy *both* of you. Besides, I *like* to see girls making it with each other. It turns me on. We'll make a great threesome!"

Lucy swirled and began advancing on Andy, her knife outstretched. "No, we *won't* make a great threesome! We don't *want* you and you're going to *leave*!"

Andy leaped out of his chair and grabbed Lucy's knife hand. He twisted the knife away as he slid smoothly behind her. One brawny forearm encircled her neck, immobilizing her. He held the knife to her throat. "Now, that ain't no way to talk to the future father of your children," he cooed into her ear.

"Put down the knife and get away from Lucy," I said to him.

Andy glanced at me. When he'd leapt for Lucy, his rifle had clattered to the floor. I had just as quickly scooped it up. Now I pointed it at him.

He chuckled. "Oh, Valerie, you don't want to do anything hasty with that. You could hurt Lucy."

"Just step away from her and leave us alone and no one will get hurt."

Andy released Lucy and stepped away from her, both arms in the air, knife still in his hand. "Okay, I'm stepping away from Lucy. But I'm not leaving."

Andy began walking slowly toward me. "We're going to come to an understanding tonight about how it's going to be from now on between us."

"There isn't going to be any 'from now on between us.' You're going to leave or I'm going to kill you."

Andy chuckled, still advancing. "Oh, Valerie, Valerie. You're not going to kill me. You're a woman, and a woman *needs* a man." Then he paused, considering me. His eyes narrowed. "Since there's two of you girls here, I don't know if I need a bitch like *you!*" Andy lunged at me, knife extended.

I pulled the trigger and the rifle stuttered. The bullets tore into Andy's chest and threw him back against the kitchen counter. He slid to the floor, leaving a smear of blood behind on the counter.

"Yeah," I said to his corpse. "A woman needs a man...like a fish needs a bicycle."

✧

Lucy and I each took an arm and we dragged Andy out the back door and down to the grove of woods. Lucy had a shovel in her free hand, I had Andy's assault rifle in mine. We took turns digging a shallow grave and then we rolled him in. I tossed his assault rifle with the banana clip in on top of him and then we covered him up. Lucy found a good-sized stone and placed it at the grave's head. I wrote "Andy" on it with the waterproof Magic Marker I used for these things. We owed Andy that much.

Then I stood with Lucy and put my arm around her shoulder and we looked down at the freshly turned dirt of Andy's grave. Our faces and blouses were drenched from the sweat of our digging. A breeze came up from the stream and cooled us.

"I hope he's the last man," Lucy said.

I glanced along the row of graves stretching out beyond Andy's in a line, every single one filled with someone who had underestimated us. Each one had a stone with a man's name on it, though the oldest names had long since faded from their stones. Neither of us could remember who they might have been.

"Yes," I agreed. "I hope he's the last of them."

I pulled Lucy close and kissed her. Then we turned and walked back toward the house, her hand in mine. The beef stew still bubbled on the fire and its scent filled my nostrils. It smelled like home.

Copyright © 2023 by Eric Leif Davin.

April 2023

Gardner Raymond Dozois (July 23, 1947— May 27, 2018) was an American science fiction author and editor. He was the founding editor of The Year's Best Science Fiction *anthologies (1984–2018) and was editor of* Asimov's Science Fiction *magazine (1984–2004), garnering multiple Hugo and Locus Awards for those works almost every year. He also won the Nebula Award for Best Short Story twice.*

Jack Dann has written or edited over seventy-five books, including the international bestseller The Memory Cathedral, The Rebel, The Silent, Junction, *and* The Man Who Melted. *He is a recipient of the Nebula Award, the World Fantasy Award, the Australian Aurealis Award (three times), the Ditmar Award (five times), the Peter McNamara Achievement Award and also the Peter McNamara Convenors' Award for Excellence, the Shirley Jackson Award, and the Premios Gilgames de Narrativa Fantastica award. He has also been honoured by the Mark Twain Society (Esteemed Knight).*

Michael Swanwick is the recipient of the Nebula, Theodore Sturgeon, and World Fantasy Awards and five Hugo Awards. His recent novel, The Iron Dragon's Mother, *completes a trilogy begun twenty-five years ago with* The Iron Dragon's Daughter. *Just out is* City Under the Stars, *co-authored with the late Gardner Dozois.*

TOURING

by Gardner Dozois, Jack Dann, and Michael Swanwick

The four-seater Beechwood Bonanza dropped from a gray sky to the cheerless winter runway of Fargo Airport. Tires touched pavement, screeched, and the single-engine plane taxied to a halt. It was seven o'clock in the morning, February 3, 1959.

Buddy Holly duck-walked down the wing and hopped to the ground. It had been a long and grueling flight; his bones ached, his eyes were gritty behind the large, plastic-framed glasses, and he felt stale and curiously depressed. Overnight bag in one hand, laundry sack in the other, he stood beside Ritchie Valens for a moment, looking for their contact. White steam curled from their nostrils. Brown grass poked out of an old layer of snow beside the runway. Somewhere a dog barked, flat and far away.

Behind the hurricane fence edging the field, a stocky man waved both hands overhead. Valens nodded, and Holly hefted his bags. Behind them, J. P. Richardson grunted as he leaped down from the plane.

They walked toward the man across the tarmac, their feet crunching over patches of dirty ice.

"Jack Blemings," the man rasped as he came up to meet them. "I manage the dance hall and the hotel in Moorhead." Thin mustache, thin lips, cheeks going to jowl—Holly had met this man a thousand times before: the stogie in his mouth was inevitable; the sporty plaid hat nearly so. Blemings stuck out a hand, and Holly shuffled his bags awkwardly, trying to free his own hand.

"Real pleased to meet you, Buddy," Blemings said. His hand was soggy and boneless. "Real pleased to meet a real artist."

He gestured them into a show-room new '59 Cadillac. It dipped on its springs as Richardson gingerly collapsed into the backseat. Starting the engine, Blemings leaned over the seat for more introductions. Richardson was blowing his nose but hastily transferred the silk handker-chief into his other hand so that they could shake. His delighted-to-meet-you expression lasted as long as the handshake, then the animation went out of him, and his face slumped back into lines of dull fatigue.

The Cadillac jerked into motion with an ostentatious squeal of rubber. Once across the Red River, which still ran steaming with gunmetal predawn mist, they were out of North Dakota and into Moorhead, Minnesota. The streets of Moorhead were empty—not so much as a garbage truck out yet. "Sleepy little burg," Valens commented. No one responded. They pulled up to an undistinguished six-story brick hotel in the heart of town.

The hotel lobby was cavernous and gloomy, inhabited only by a few tired-looking, potted rubber plants. As they walked past a grouping of battered armchairs and sagging sofas toward the shadowy information desk in the back, dust puffed at their feet from the faded gray carpet. An unmoving ceiling fan cast thin-armed shadows across the room, and everything smelled of old cigar butts, dead flies, and trapped sunshine.

The front desk was as deserted as the rest of the lobby. Blemings slammed the bell angrily until a balding, bored-looking man appeared from the back, moving as though he were swimming through syrup. As the desk clerk doled out room keys, still moving like a somnambulist, Blemings took the cigar out of his mouth and said, "I spoke with your road manager, must've been right after you guys left the Surf Ballroom. Needed his okay for two acts I'm adding to the show." He paused. "S'awright with you, hey?"

Holly shrugged. "It's your show," he said.

✧

Holly unlaced one shoe, letting it drop heavily to the floor. His back ached, and the long, sleepless flight had made his suit rumpled and sour smelling. One last chore and he could sleep: he picked up the bedside telephone and dialed the hotel operator for an outside line so that he could call his wife, Maria, in New York and tell her that he had arrived safely.

The phone was dead; the switchboard must be closed down. He sighed and bent over to pick up his shoe again.

Eight or nine men were standing around the lobby when Holly stepped out of the elevator, husky fellows, southern boys by the look of them. Two were at the front desk, making demands of the clerk, who responded by spreading his arms wide and rolling his eyes upward.

Waiting his turn for service, Holly leaned back against the counter, glancing about. He froze in disbelief. Against all logic, all possibility, Elvis Presley himself was standing not six yards away on the gray carpet. For an instant Holly struggled with amazement. Then a second glance told him the truth.

Last year Elvis had been drafted into the army, depriving his fans of his presence and creating a ready market for those who could imitate him. A legion of Presley impersonators had crowded into the welcoming spotlights of stages across the country, trying vainly to fill the gap left by the King of Rock and Roll.

This man, though, he stood out. At first glance he was Elvis. An instant later you saw that he was twenty years too old and as much as forty pounds overweight. There were dissolute lines under his eyes and a weary, dissipated expression on his face. The rigors of being on the road had undone his ducktail so that his hair was an untidy mess, hanging down over his forehead and curling over his ears. He wore a sequined shirt, now wrinkled and sweaty, and a suede jacket.

Holly went over to introduce himself. "Hi," he said, "I guess you're playing to-night's show."

The man ignored his out-thrust hand. Dark, haunted eyes bored into Holly's. "I don't know what kind of game you're playing, son," he said. A soft Tennessee accent underlay his words. "But I'm packing a piece, and I know how to use it." His hand darted inside his jacket and emerged holding an ugly-looking .38.

Involuntarily Holly sucked in his breath. He slowly raised his hands shoulder high and backed away. "Hey, it's okay," he said. "I was just trying to be friendly." The man's eyes followed his retreat suspiciously, and he didn't reholster the gun until Holly was back at the front desk.

The desk clerk was free now. Holly slid three bills across the counter, saying, "Change please." From the corner of his eye, he saw the imitation Elvis getting into the elevator, surrounded by his entourage. They were solicitous, almost subservient. One patted the man's back as he shakily recounted his close call. *Poor old man*, Holly thought pityingly. The man was really cracking under the pressures of the road. He'd be lucky to last out the tour.

In the wooden booth across the lobby, Holly dumped his change on the ledge below the phone. He dialed the operator for long distance. The earpiece buzzed, made clicking noises, then filled with harsh, actinic static, and the clicking grew faster and louder. Holly jiggled the receiver, racked the phone angrily.

Another flood of musicians and crew coursed through the lobby. Stepping from the booth, ruefully glancing back at the phone, Holly collided with a small woman in a full-length mink. "Oof," she said and then reached out and gave him a squeeze to show there were no hard feelings. A mobile, hoydenish face grinned up at him.

"Hey, sport," she said brightly. "I *love* that bow tie. And those glasses!—Jesus, you look just like Buddy Holly!"

"I know," he said wryly. But she was gone. He trudged back to the elevators. Then something caught his eye, and he swung about, openly staring.

Was that a *man* she was talking to? My God, he had hair down to his shoulders!

Trying not to stare at this amazing apparition, he stepped into the elevator. Back in his room, he stopped only long enough to pick up his bag of laundry before heading out again. He was going to have to go outside the hotel to find a working phone anyway; he might as well fight down his weariness, hunt up a Laundromat, and get his laundry done.

The lobby was empty when he returned through it, and he couldn't even find the desk clerk to ask where the nearest Laundromat was. Muttering under his breath, Holly trudged out of the hotel.

Outside, the sun was shining brilliantly but without warmth from out of a hard, high blue sky. There was still no traffic, no one about on the street, and Holly walked along through an early-morning silence broken only by the squeaking of his sneakers, past closed-up shops and shuttered brownstone houses. He found a Laundromat after a few more blocks, and although it was open, there was no one in there either, not even the inevitable elderly Negro attendant. The rows of unused washing machines glinted dully in the dim light cast by a flyspecked bulb. Shrugging, he dumped his clothes into a machine. The change machine didn't work, of course, but you got used to dealing with things like that on the road, and he'd brought a handkerchief full of change with him. He got the machine going and then went out to look for a phone.

The streets were still empty, and after a few more blocks it began to get on his nerves. He'd been in hick towns before—had grown up in one—but this was the sleepiest, *deadest* damn town he'd ever seen. There was still no traffic, although there were plenty of cars parked by the curbs, and he hadn't seen another person since leaving the hotel. There weren't even any *pigeons*, for goodness sake!

There was a five-and-dime on the corner, its doors standing open. Holly poked his head inside. The lights were on, but there were no customers, no floorwalkers, no salesgirls behind the counters. True, small-town people weren't as suspicious as folk from the bigger cities—but still, this *was* a business, and it looked as if anyone could just walk in here and walk off with any of the unguarded merchandise. It was gloomy and close in the empty store, and the air was filled with dust. Holly backed out of the doorway, somehow not wanting to explore the depths of the store for the sales personnel who *must* be in there somewhere.

A slight wind had come up now, it flicked grit against his face and blew bits of scrap paper down the empty street.

He found a phone on the next corner, hunted through his handkerchief for a dime while the wind snatched at the edges of the fabric. The phone buzzed and clicked at him again, and this time there was the faint, high wailing of wind in the wires, an eerie, desolate sound that always made him think of ghosts wandering alone through the darkness. The next phone he found was also dead, and the next.

Uneasily, he picked up his laundry and headed back to the hotel.

The desk clerk was spreading his hands wide in a gesture of helpless abnegation of responsibility when the fat southerner in the sequined shirt leaned forward, poked a hard finger into the clerk's chest, and said softly, "You know who I am, son?"

"Why, of course I do, Mr. Presley," the clerk said nervously. "Yessir, of course I do, sir."

"You say you know who I am, son," Elvis said in a cottony voice that slowly mounted in volume. "If you know who I am, then you *know* why I don't have to stay in a goddamned flophouse like this! Isn't that right? Would you give your mother a room like that? You know goddamned well you wouldn't. Just what are you people thinking of? I'm *Elvis Presley,* and you'd give me a room like that!"

Elvis was bellowing now, his face grown red and mottled, his features assuming that look of sulky, sneering meanness that had thrilled millions. His eyes were hard and bright as glass. As the frightened clerk shrank back, his hands held up now as much in terror as in supplication, Elvis suddenly began to change. He looked at the clerk sadly, as if pitying him, and said, "Son, do you know who I am?"

"Yessir," whispered the clerk.

"Then can't you see it?" asked Elvis.

"See what, sir?"

"That I'm *chosen!* Are you an atheist? Are you a goddamned atheist?" Elvis pounded on the desk and barked, "I'm the star, I've been given that, and you can't soil it, you atheist bastard! You *sonovabitch!*"

Now that was the worst thing he could call anyone, and he never, almost never used it, for his mother, may she rest in peace, was holy. *She* had believed in him, had told him that the Lord had chosen *him*, that as long as he sang and believed, the Lord would take care of him. Like this? Is this the way He was going to take care of me?

"*I'm* the star, and I could *buy* this hotel out of my spare change! Buy it, you hear that?" And even as he spoke, the incongruity of the whole situation hit him, really hit him hard for the first time. It was as though his mind had suddenly cleared after a long, foggy daze, as if the scales had fallen from his eyes.

Elvis stopped shouting and stumbled back from the desk, frightened now, fears and suspicions flooding in on him like the sea. What was he doing *here?* Dammit, he was the King! He'd made his comeback, and he'd played to capacity crowds at the biggest concert halls in the country. And now he couldn't even remember how he'd gotten here—he'd been at Graceland, and then everything had gotten all foggy and confused, and the next thing he knew he was climbing out of the bus in front of this hotel with the roadies and the rest of the band. Even if he'd agreed to play this one-horse town, it would have to have been for charity. That's it, it had to be for charity. But then where were the reporters, the TV crews? His coming here would be the biggest damn thing that had ever happened in Moorhead, Minnesota. Why weren't there any screaming crowds being held back by police?

"What in hell's going on here?" Elvis shouted. He snatched out his revolver and gestured to his two bodyguards to close up on either side of him. His gaze darted wildly about the lobby as he tried to look into every corner at once. "Keep your eyes open! There's something funny—"

At that moment Jack Blemings stepped out of his office, shut the door smoothly behind him, and sauntered across the musty old carpet toward them. "Something wrong here, Mr. Presley?"

"Damn *right* there is," Elvis raged, taking a couple of steps toward Blemings and brandishing his gun. "You know how many *years* it's been since I played a tank town like this? I don't know what in hell the Colonel was thinking of to send me down here. I—"

Smiling blandly and ignoring the gun, Blemings reached out and touched Elvis on the chest.

Elvis shuddered and took a lurching step backward, his eyes glazing over. He shook his head, looked foggily around the lobby, glanced down at the gun in his hand as though noticing it for the first time, then holstered it absentmindedly. "Time's the show tonight?" he mumbled.

"About eight, Mr. Presley," Blemings answered, smiling. "You've got plenty of time to relax before then."

Elvis looked around the lobby again, running a hand through his greased-back hair. "Anything to do around here?" he asked, a hint of the old sneer returning.

"We got a real nice bar, right over there, the other side of the lobby," Blemings said.

"I don't drink," Elvis said sullenly.

"Well, then," Blemings added brightly, "we got some real nice pinball machines in that bar, too."

Shaking his head, Elvis turned and moved away across the lobby, taking his entourage with him.

Blemings went back into his office.

☼

J. P. Richardson had unpacked the scotch and was going for ice when he saw the whore. There was no mistaking what she was. She was dressed in garish gypsy clothes with ungodly amounts of jewelry about her neck and wrists. Beneath a light blouse her breasts swayed freely—she wasn't even wearing a bra. Richardson didn't have to be told how she had earned the mink coat that was draped over one arm.

"Hey, little sister," Richardson said softly. He was still wearing the white suit that was his onstage trademark, his "Big Bopper" outfit. He looked good in it and knew it. "Are you available?"

"You talking to me, honey?" She spoke defiantly, almost jeeringly, but something in her stance, her bold stare, told him she was ready for almost anything. He discreetly slid a twenty from a jacket pocket, smiled, and nodded.

"I'd like to make an appointment," he said, slipping the folded bill into her hand. "That is, if you *are* available now."

She stared from him to the bill and back, a look of utter disbelief on her face. Then, suddenly, she grinned. "Why, 'course I'm available, sugar. What's your room number? Gimme ten minutes to stash my coat, and I'll be right there."

"It's room four eleven." Richardson watched her flounce down the hall, and, despite some embarrassment, was pleased. There was a certain tawdry charm to her. Probably ruts like a mink, he told himself. He went back to his room to wait.

The woman went straight to the hotel bar, slapped the bill down, and shouted, "Hey, kids, pony up! The drinks are on Janis!"

There was a vague stirring, and three lackluster men eddied toward the bar.

Janis looked about, saw that the place was almost empty. A single drunk sat walleyed at a table, holding onto its edges with clenched hands to keep from falling over. To the rear, almost lost in gloom, a big stud was playing pinball. Two unfriendly types, who looked like bodyguards, stood nearby, protecting him from the empty tables. Otherwise—nothing. "Shoulda taken the fat dude up on his offer," she grumbled. "There's nothing happening *here*." Then, to the bartender, "Make mine a whiskey sour."

She took a gulp of her drink, feeling sorry for herself. The clatter of pinball bells ceased briefly as the stud lost his ball. He slammed the side of the machine viciously with one hand. She swiveled on her stool to look at him.

"Damn," she said to the bartender. "You know, from this angle that dude looks just like *Elvis*."

☼

Buddy Holly finished adjusting his bow tie, reached for a comb, then stopped in mid-motion. He stared about the tiny dressing room with its cracked mirror and bare light bulbs and asked himself, *How did I get here?*

It was no idle, existential question. He really did not know. The last thing he remembered was entering his hotel room and collapsing on the bed. Then—here. There was nothing in between.

A rap at the door. Blemings stuck his head in, the stench of his cigar permeating the room. "Everything okay in here, Mr. Holly?"

"Well," Holly began. But he went no further. What could he say? "How long before I go on?"

"Plenty of time. You might want to catch the opener, though—good act. On in ten."

"Thanks."

Blemings left, not quite shutting the door behind him. Holly studied his face in the mirror. It looked haggard and unresponsive. He flashed a toothy smile but did not feel it. God, he was tired. Being on the road was going to kill him. There had to be a way off this treadmill.

The woman from the hotel leaned into his room. "Hey, Ace—you seen that Blemings motherfucker anywhere?"

Holly's jaw dropped. To hear that kind of language from a woman—from a *white* woman. "He just went by," he said weakly.

"*Shit!*" She was gone.

Her footsteps echoed in the hallway, swallowed up by silence. And that was ... *wrong*. There should be the murmur and nervous bustle of acts preparing to go on, last-minute errands being run, equipment being tested. Holly peered into the corridor—empty.

To one side, the hall dead-ended into a metal door with a red EXIT sign overhead. Holly went the other way, toward the stage. Just as he reached the wings, the audience burst into prolonged, almost frenzied applause. The Elvis impersonator was striding onstage. It was a great crowd.

But the wings were empty. No stagehands or gofers, no idlers, nobody preparing for the next set.

"Elvis" spread his legs wide and crouched low, his thick lips curling in a sensual sneer. He was wearing a gold lamé jumpsuit, white scarf about his neck. He moved his guitar loosely, adjusting the strap, then gave his band the downbeat.

Well it's one for the money
Two for the show
Three to get ready
Now go, cat, go!

And he was off and running into a brilliant rendition of "Blue Suede Shoes." Not an easy song to do, because the lyrics were laughable. It relied entirely on the music, and it took a real entertainer to make it work.

This guy had it all, though. The jumps, gyrations, and forward thrusts of the groin were stock stuff—but somehow he made them look right. He played the audience too, and his control was perfect. Holly could see shadowy shapes beyond the glare of the footlights, moving in a more than sexual frenzy, was astonished by their rapturous screams. All this in the first minutes of the set.

He's good, Holly marveled. Why was he wasting that kind of talent on a novelty act? There was a tug at his arm, and he shrugged it off.

The tug came again. "Hey, man," somebody said, and he turned to find himself again facing the woman. Their eyes met, and her expression changed oddly, becoming a mixture of bewilderment and outright fear. "Jesus God," she said in awe. "You're Buddy Holly!"

"You've already told me that," he said, irritated. He wanted to watch the man on stage—who *was* he, anyway?—not be distracted by this foul-mouthed and probably not very clean woman.

"No, I mean it—you're *really* Buddy Holly. And that dude on stage"—she pointed—"he's Elvis Presley."

"It's a good act," Holly admitted. "But it wouldn't fool my grandmother. That good ol' boy's forty if he's a day."

"Look," she said. "I'm Janis Joplin. I guess that don't mean nothing to you, but—hey, lemme show ya something." She tried to tug him away from the stage.

"I want to see the man's act," he said mildly.

"It won't take a minute, man. And it's important. I swear it. It's—you just gotta see it, is all."

There was no denying her. She led him away, down the corridor to the metal door with its red EXIT sign, and threw it open. "Look!"

He squinted into a dull, winter evening. Across a still, car-choked parking lot was a row of faded, brick buildings. A featureless, gray sky overhung all. "There used ta be a lot more out here," Janis babbled. "All the rest of the town. It all went away. Can you dig it, man? It just all—went away."

Holly shivered. This woman was crazy! "Look, Miss Joplin," he began. Then the buildings winked out of existence.

He blinked. The buildings had not faded away—they had simply ceased to be. As crisply and sharply as if somebody had flipped a switch. He opened his mouth; shut it again.

Janis was talking quietly, fervently. "I don't know what it is, man, but something *very weird* is going down here." Everything beyond the parking lot was a smooth, even gray. Janis started to speak again, stopped, moistened her lips. She looked suddenly hesitant and oddly embarrassed. "I mean, like, I don't know how to break this to ya, Buddy, but you're *dead. You* bought it in a plane crash way back in 'fifty-nine."

"This *is* 'fifty-nine," Holly said absently, looking out across the parking lot, still dazed, her words not really sinking in. As he watched, the cars snapped out of existence row by row, starting with the farthest row, working inward to the nearest. Only the asphalt lot itself remained, and a few bits of litter lying between the painted slots. Holly's groin tightened, and as fear broke through astonishment, he registered Janis's words and felt rage grow alongside fear.

"No, honey," Janis was saying, "I hate to tell ya, but this is 1970." She paused, looking uncertain. "Or maybe not. Ol' Elvis looks a deal older than I remember him being. We must be in the future or something, huh? Some kinda sci-fi trip like that, like on 'Star Trek'? You think we—"

But Holly had swung around ferociously, cutting her off. "*Stop it!*" he said. "I don't know what's going on, what kind of trick you people are trying to play on me, or how you're doing all these things, but I'm not going to put up with any more of—"

Janis put her hand on Holly's shoulder; it felt hot and small and firm, like a child's hand. "Hey, listen," Janis said quietly, cutting him off. "I know this is hard for you to accept, and it is pretty heavy stuff… but, Buddy, you're *dead. I* mean, really, you are… It was about ten years ago, you were on tour, right? And your plane *crashed*, spread you *all* over some farmer's field. It was in all the goddamn papers, you and Ritchie Valens and …." She paused, startled, and then grinned. "And that fat dude at the hotel, that must've been the *Big Bopper*. Wow! Man, if I'd known *that* I might've taken him up on it. You were all on your way to some diddly-shit hicktown like …." She stopped, and when she started to speak again, she had gone pale "…like Moorhead, Minnesota. Oh, Christ, I think it was Moorhead. Oh, boy, is that spooky…"

Holly sighed. His anger had suddenly collapsed, leaving him feeling hollow and confused and tired. He blinked away a memory that wasn't a memory of torn-up black ground and twisted shards of metal. "I don't *feel* dead," he said. His stomach hurt.

"You don't *look* dead either," Janis reassured him. "But, honey, I mean, you really *were*."

They stood staring out across the now vacant parking lot, a cold, cinder-smelling wind tugging at their clothes and hair. At last, Janis said, her brassy voice gone curiously shy, "You got real famous, ya know, after … afterward. You even influenced, like, the *Beatles* …. Shit, I forgot!—I guess you don't even know who they *are*, do you?" She paused uncomfortably, then said, "Anyway, honey, you got real famous."

"*That's nice,*" Holly said dully.

The parking lot disappeared. Holly gasped and flinched back. Everything was gone. Three concrete steps with an iron pipe railing led down from the door into a vast, unmoving nothingness.

"What a trip," Janis muttered. "What a trip …"

They stared at the oozing gray nothingness until it seemed to Holly that it was creeping closer and then shuddering, he slammed the door shut.

Holly found himself walking down the corridor, going no place in particular, his flesh still crawling.

Janis tagged along after him, talking anxiously. "Ya know, I can't even really remember how I got to this burg. I was in L.A. the last I remember, but then everything gets all foggy. I thought it was the booze, but now I dunno."

"Maybe you're dead, too," Holly said almost absentmindedly.

Janis paled, but a strange kind of excitement shot through her face under the fear, and she began to talk faster and faster. "Yeah, honey, maybe I am. I thought of that too, man, once I saw you. Maybe whoever's behind all this are *magicians*, man, black magicians, and they conjured us all *up*." She laughed a slightly hysterical laugh. "And you wanna know another weird thing? I can't find any of my sidemen here or the roadies or *anybody*, ya know? Valens and the Bopper don't seem to be here either. All of 'em were at the hotel, but backstage here it's just you and me and Elvis and that motherfucker Blemings. It's like *they're* not really interested in the rest of them, right? They were just window dressing, man, but now they don't need 'em anymore, and so they sent them *back*. We're the headline acts, sweetie. Everybody else *they* vanished, just like they vanished the fucking parking lot, right? Right?"

"I don't know," Holly said. He needed time to think. Time alone.

"Or, hey—how about this? Maybe you're *not* dead. Maybe we got nabbed by flying saucers, and these aliens faked our deaths, right? Snatched you out of your plane, maybe. And they put us together here—wherever here is—not because they dig rock. Shit, they probably can't even *understand* it—but to study us and all that kinda shit. Or maybe it *is* 1959; maybe we got kidnapped by some time-traveler who's a big rock freak. Or maybe it's a million years in the future, and they've got us all *taped*, see? And they want to hear us, so they put on the tape, and we *think* we're here, only we're not. It's all a recording. Hey?"

"I don't *know*."

Blemings came walking down the corridor, cigar trailing a thin plume of smoke behind him. "Janis, honey! I've been beating the bushes for you, sweetie pie. You're on in two."

"Listen, motherfuck," Janis said angrily. "I want a few answers from you!" Blemings reached out and touched her hand. Her eyes went blank, and she meekly allowed him to lead her away.

"A real trouper, hey?" Blemings said cheerfully.

"Hey!" Holly said. But they were already gone.

✧

Elvis laid down his guitar, whipped the scarf from his neck, and mopped his brow with it. He kissed the scarf and threw it into the crowd. The screams reached crescendo pitch as the little girls fought over its possession. With a jaunty wave of one hand, he walked offstage.

In the wings, he doubled over, breathing heavily. Sweat ran out of every pore in his body. He reached out a hand, but no one put a towel in it. He looked up angrily.

The wings were empty, save for a kid in big glasses. Elvis gestured weakly toward a nearby piece of terry cloth. "Towel," he gasped, and the kid fetched it.

Toweling off his face, Elvis threw back his head, began to catch his breath. He let the cloth slip to his shoulders and for the first time got a good look at the kid standing before him. "You're Buddy Holly," he said. He was proud of how calmly it came out.

"A lot of people have told me that today," Holly said.

The crowd roared, breaking off their conversation. They turned to look. Janis was dancing onstage from the opposite side. Shadowy musicians to the rear were laying down a hot, bluesy beat. She grabbed the microphone, laughed into it.

"Well! Ain't this a kick in the ass? Yeah. Real nice, real nice." There were anxious lines about her eyes, but most of the audience wouldn't be able to see that. "Ya know, I been thinking a lot about life lately. 'Deed I have. And I been thinkin' how it's like one a dem ole-time blues songs. Ya know? I mean, it *hurts* so bad, and it feels so *good!*" The crowd screamed approval. The band kept laying down the rhythm. "So, I got a song here that kind of proves my point."

She swung an arm up and then down, giving the band the beat, and launched into "Heart and Soul."

"Well?" Elvis said. "Give me the message."

Holly was staring at the woman on-stage. "I never heard anyone sing like that before," he murmured. Then, "I'm sorry—I don't know what you mean, Mr. Presley."

"Call me Elvis," he said automatically. He felt disappointed. There had been odd signs and omens, and now the spirits of departed rock stars were appearing before him—there really ought to be a message. But it was clear the kid was telling the truth; he looked scared and confused.

Elvis turned on a winning smile and impulsively plucked a ring from one of his fingers. It was a good ring; lots of diamonds and rubies. He thrust it into Holly's hands. "Here, take this. I don't want the goddamned thing anymore, anyway."

Holly squinted at the ring quizzically. "Well, put it on," Elvis snapped. When Holly had complied, he said, "Maybe you'd better tell me what you *do* know."

Holly told his story. "I understand now," Elvis said. "We're caught in a snare and delusion of Satan."

"You think so?" Holly looked doubtful.

"Squat down." Elvis hunkered down on the floor, and after an instant's hesitation, Holly followed suit. "I've got powers," Elvis explained. "The power to heal—stuff like that. Now me and my momma, we were always close. Real close. So, she'll be able to help us, if we ask her."

"Your mother?"

"She's in Heaven," Elvis said matter-of-factly.

"Oh," Holly said weakly.

"Now join hands and concentrate real *hard*."

Holly felt embarrassed and uncomfortable. Since he was a good Baptist, which he certainly tried to be, the idea of a backstage seance seemed blasphemous. But Elvis, whether he was the real item or not, scared him. Elvis's eyes were screwed shut, and he was saying, "Momma. Can you hear me, Momma?" over and over in a fanatic drone.

The seance seemed to go on for hours, Holly suffering through it in mute misery, listening as well as he could to Janis, as she sang her way through number after amazing number. And finally, she was taking her last bows, crowing, "Thank you, thank you," at the crowd.

There was a cough at his shoulder and a familiar stench of tobacco. Holly looked up. "You're on," Blemings said. He touched Holly's shoulder.

Without transition, Holly found himself onstage. The audience was noisy and enthusiastic, a good bunch. A glance to the rear, he saw that the backup musicians were not his regular sidemen. They stood in shadow, and he could not see their faces.

But the applause was long and loud; it crept up under his skin and into his veins, and he knew he had to play *something*. "Peggy Sue," he called to the musicians, hoping they knew the number. When he started playing his guitar, they were right with him. Tight. It was a helluva good backup band; their playing had bone and sinew to it. The audience was on its feet now, bouncing to the beat.

He gave them "Rave On," "Maybe Baby," "Words of Love," and "That'll Be the Day," and the audience yelped and howled like wild beasts, but when he called out "Not Fade Away" to the musicians, the crowd quieted, and he felt a special, higher tension come into the hall. The band did a good, strong intro, and he began singing.

I wanna tell you how it's gonna be
You're gonna give your love to me

He had never felt the music take hold of him this immediately, this strongly, and he felt a surge of exhilaration that seemed to instantly communicate itself to the audience and be reflected back at him redoubled, bringing them all up to a deliriously high level of intensity. Never had he performed better. He glanced offstage, saw that Janis was swaying to the beat, slapping a hand against her thigh. Even Elvis was following the music, caught up in it, grinning broadly and clapping his ring-studded hands.

For love is love and not fade away.

Somewhere to the rear, one of the ghostly backup musicians was blowing a blues harmonica, as good as any he'd ever heard.

There was a flash of scarlet, and Janis had run onstage. She grabbed a free mic and joined him in the chorus. When they reached the second verse, they turned to face each other and began trading off lines. Janis sang:

My love bigger than a Cadillac

and he responded. His voice was flat next to hers. He couldn't give the words the emotional twist she could, but their voices synched, they meshed, they worked together perfectly.

When the musical break came, somebody threw Janis a tambourine so she could stay onstage, and she nabbed it out of the air. Somebody else kicked a bottle of Southern Comfort across the stage; she stopped it with her foot, lifted it, and downed a big slug. Holly was leaping into the air, doing splits, using every trick of an old rocker's repertoire, and miraculously he felt he could keep on doing so forever, could stretch the breakout to infinity if he tried.

Janis beckoned widely toward the wings. "Come on out," she cried into the microphone. "Come on."

To a rolling avalanche of applause, Elvis strode onstage. He grabbed a guitar and strapped it on, taking a stance beside Holly. "You don't mind?" he mumbled.

Holly grinned.

They went into the third verse in unison. Standing between the other two, Holly felt alive and holy and—better than either alive or holy—*right*. They were his brother and sister. They were in tune; he could not have sworn which body was his.

Well, love is love and not fade away

Elvis was wearing another scarf. He whipped it off, mopped his brow, and went to the footlights to dangle it into the crowd. Then he retreated as fast as if he'd been bitten by a snake.

Holly saw Elvis talking to Janis, frantically waving an arm at the crowd beyond the footlights. She ignored him, shrugging off his words. Holly squinted, could not make out a thing in the gloom.

Curious, he duck-walked to the edge of the stage and peered beyond.

Half the audience was gone. As he watched, the twenty people farthest from the stage snapped out of existence. Then another twenty. And another.

The crowd noise continued undiminished, the clapping and whooping and whistling, but the audience was *gone* now—except for Blemings, who sat alone in the exact center of the empty theater. He was smiling faintly at them, a smile that could have meant anything, and as Holly watched, he began softly, politely, to applaud.

Holly retreated backstage, pale, still playing automatically. Only Janis was singing now.

Not fade away

Holly glanced back at the musicians, saw first one, then another, cease to exist. Unreality was closing in on them. He stared into Elvis's face, and for an instant, saw mirrored there the fear he felt.

Then Elvis threw back his head and laughed and was singing into his mic again. Holly gawked at him in disbelief.

But the *music* was right, and the *music* was good, and while all the rest—audience, applause, someplace to go when the show was over—was nice, it wasn't necessary. Holly glanced both ways and saw that he was not the only one to understand this. He rejoined the chorus.

Janis was squeezing the microphone tight, singing, when the last sideman blinked out. The only backup now came from Holly's guitar—Elvis had discarded his. She knew it was only a matter of minutes before the nothingness reached them, but it didn't really matter. *The music's all that matters*, she thought. *It's all that made any of it tolerable, anyway.* She sang.

Not fade away

Elvis snapped out. She and Holly kept on singing.

If anyone out there is listening, she thought. *If you can read my mind or some futuristic bullshit like that—I just want you to know that I'd do this again anytime. You want me, you got me.*

Holly disappeared. Janis realized that she had only seconds to go herself, and she put everything she had into the last repetition of the line. She wailed out her soul, and a little bit more. *Let it echo after I'm gone*, she thought. *Let it hang on thin air*. And as the last fractional breath of music left her mouth, she felt something seize her, prepare to turn her off.

Not fade away

It had been a good session.

Copyright © 1981 by Gardner Dozois, Jack Dann, and Michael Swanwick. First appeared in Pentrouse, *April 2021.*

EDITED BY
OGHENECHOVWE DONALD EKPEKI
EUGEN BACON
MILTON DAVIS

THE YEAR'S BEST AFRICAN SPECULATIVE FICTION 2022

Sequel to the award-winning anthology
(World Fantasy Award)

May 2023

Yefim Zozulya is one of the greatest fabulist of his generation, known for writing dark, speculative, and macabre short fiction in 1920s Russia. He was prolific, his works published in popular literary magazines. His short story "The Tale of Ak and Humanity" directly inspired Zamyatin's We *and may be the foundational work of the anti-utopian genre.*

Alex Shvartsman is the author of Kakistocracy *(2023),* The Middling Affliction *(2022), and* Eridani's Crown *(2019) fantasy novels. Over 120 of his stories have appeared in* Analog, Nature, Strange Horizons, *etc. He won the WSFA Small Press Award for Short Fiction and was a three-time finalist for the Canopus Award for Excellence in Interstellar Fiction. His translations from Russian have appeared in* F&SF, Clarkesworld, Tor.com, Asimov's, *etc. Alex has edited over a dozen anthologies, including the long-running Unidentified Funny Objects series.*

CAIN AND ABEL

by Yefim Zozulya, translated by Alex Shvartsman

1

CAIN HAD SOME STRANGE TENDENCIES.

The downpour was heavy; it bent trees, trampled grass, and came down in long, thick, angry water funnels. The sheep huddled in a thick, inseparable mass and breathed heavily, painfully into each other's warm shivering bodies, into the wet, slippery wool.

The frightened calls of birds sounded in the pounding, whipping darkness, as the downpour swept them from under the cover of leaves.

Even the solid hut, made by Cain's steady hands out of leather, sod, and twigs, slipped and flattened, water trickling in from one side.

Adam lay in the hut, covered only by a pair of sheepskins, and bleated in a long, uncertain, monotonic howl. The howls intensified whenever the darkness was torn asunder by lightning, followed by the deafening rumble of thunder.

Adam raised his head anxiously, his half-simian, overgrown eyes staring at the familiar fields that now looked strange and foreign and blue. He howled even more despondently and cowered under the sheepskins.

Eve remained silent. Her big, white, sly brow was furrowed in concern. Her thin lips were pressed tight. Her chest was heaving rapidly, and her thick strong fingers ran through the wavy hair of Abel, who lay at her feet.

She caressed Abel, but didn't notice him, just as she didn't notice Adam. She prayed with the eternal prayer of a mother: a silent prayer frozen in the whites of her alert, wide-open eyes.

"Lord," she prayed, "the fields are dark and terrifying. There's fire, water, and thunder. And Cain, my son, is missing! Please save him from the fire, the water, and the thunder!"

When the downpour abated somewhat, Eve asked, "Abel, where's Cain?"

"He's dancing, Mom," Abel responded in his usual gentle and soft manner. "He loves to dance under thunder and rain. He jumps and bends his arms and legs."

"But where is he?"

"In the field by the forest, Mom."

The downpour weakened, and suddenly a loud, unpleasant, rough and harsh human scream could be heard through the muted susurrus of running water. The scream alternated from even and powerful to shrill and foolish. Gratuitous gaiety, an exuberant excess of strength, and the overflowing energy of a strong body and an unbridled soul could all be heard within it.

All three of them were silent.

They knew that this was Cain screaming. They'd long become accustomed to not speaking about his oddities and eccentricities. From that reticence of the first ever family, the lie of family pride had been silently born. Only Abel wanted to draw Mother's attention to the strangeness of his brother, but he knew from experience that Mother was not fond of his unkind and envious powers of observation.

When it had stopped raining and dawn had come, and the sky looked guiltily clear, and dark clouds had dispersed repentantly toward its edges, Cain's gloomy figure appeared at the hut's entrance. The streaks on his head were wet and shiny. Water dripped from his half-naked body. He was tired. His huge arms dangled along his dark, hirsute body. He was breathing heavily. And yet, he looked handsome.

A dark, violent power emanated from him. Eve, who hadn't slept all night, recalled what she'd said while filled with the soaring pride she couldn't quite understand when he was born: *I have gotten a man from the Lord.*

2
PEOPLE LEARN ABOUT EACH OTHER.

Cain was a tiller. The land was strong and indifferent. It grudgingly yielded growth. Grudgingly provided bread. Cain had to dig deep to aerate the soil before planting seeds, and the sharpened stakes he used for this purpose dulled quickly. Cain had to frequently cut down trees and make new stakes.

Once, he loosened a dense, strong tree, in hopes of felling it and breaking it up. The roots wouldn't give, holding on with incomprehensible might. Cain grew furious. His neck turned red. His enormous muscles bulged and glistened like balloons. Puffs of steam escaped from his mouth.

Sweaty, hot, and fearsome, he threw himself at the tree, bending it to the ground with a mighty effort. He wanted to lean on it but stumbled, and the tree slapped him in the face as he straightened.

Cain fell down, growling in pain.

He got up right away, screaming and crying loudly, and threw himself at the tree once more. He grasped it with bloody hands, gasping from his screams and his effort, tore the tree out of the ground by its roots, and fell alongside it onto the grass.

Abel sat nearby, herding his flock. His pose, his wavy hair and blue eyes, shone with a serene peace. He looked upon Cain's struggle and rejoiced inwardly; the spectacle even made him squeal in delight. But once he saw the terrible whites of his brother's eyes, he turned away and pretended not to notice Cain.

To further demonstrate his indifference, he even began to sing his favorite song:

I have one sheep,
And I have one more sheep,
And I have one more sheep,
And many more, and one more sheep have I.

3
MORE ABOUT THE BROTHERS' CHARACTERS.

Cain was talented, while Abel was only observant. Abel secretly trusted his brother more than he trusted himself. When Cain looked at the sky and said it would rain tomorrow, Abel was certain the rain would come, yet tried to argue for some reason. When Cain looked at a large sheep and said it would die, Abel knew that would happen, yet tried to ague again.

Cain spat contemptuously and showed his elbow, which he did with the express purpose of insulting Abel. Furious, Abel exposed himself in a disgusting manner but this type of insult didn't work; Cain would only laugh.

Cain used a stick to draw birds in the sand, and Abel liked those drawings. But whenever he wanted to take a closer look, Cain cackled rudely and unpleasantly, shoved Abel away and trampled over the drawing.

Abel was happy the time Adam grew angry with Cain, attacked him, beat him with a rock, and bit his stomach hard enough to draw blood. Overjoyed, Abel ran to the river, jumped around there and rubbed his hands, and then returned, looking humble.

Adam didn't like Cain. Eve was also outwardly cold toward him, and from this dislike for Cain Abel drew his approval, his self-worth. It was difficult for him, because he compared himself to Cain and needed such approval, but Cain didn't need it.

Nearly every day, Abel approached Cain with all sorts of proposals, and Cain almost always rejected them.

Cain dismissed them coldly and rudely, with insults and laughter. Abel, who made those proposals in order to become first in at least something, always turned out to be second, and rejected.

There was only one thing Abel never offered: his help with Cain's work, even though he took advantage of Cain's help with his own.

"Cain, help me calm down the bull so he doesn't gore me!" Abel would come to his brother, frightened.

Cain helped, and then chided Abel: "You're insignificant, weak as the dust we tread with our feet."

And with a rough laugh he showed Abel an elbow.

4
THE FIRST CONFLICT OVER PROPERTY.

Abel said to Cain: "Why do you drink milk from my cow? Drink from your own."

"This is my cow, not yours," Cain replied.

"What about that cow?" Cain pointed at another. "Is it also yours?"

"That one's mine too. I will drink milk from that cow if I want to."

Abel fell into a frightened silence.

Cain laughed unpleasantly, and then suddenly uttered a terrible phrase, one that still makes people groan. Most importantly, he said it lightly, laughing, almost mockingly:

"Abel, let's divide the world between us."

He was clearly joking, but Abel took the offer seriously.

"Yes, let's divide it! The flocks will be mine, and the land can be yours."

"Fine." Cain laughed.

Abel drove the flocks into the field, and Cain shouted after him, laughing. "You're treading upon my land!'

Abel stopped, thought anxiously, and came up with a retort: "The clothes you're wearing, aren't they made from the skins of my sheep?"

"Get off my land!" Cain laughed.

"Take off the clothes made from my sheep," Abel shouted seriously and anxiously.

He suddenly ran toward Cain, white from anger and fear, trembling with rage, gasping for breath. His face was screwed up, his mouth twisted. He burst into tears and shouted terribly: "My sheep! My cows! My goatlings! My calves! My bulls! Mine! Mine! Mine! Do you hear, Cain, mine…!"

He was disgusting, and Cain pushed him away with his hand, laughing coldly.

Abel grabbed a stone and swung it, but Cain ripped the stone from his hands. A fight broke out.

Wearing torn skins over their half-naked bodies, they chased each other across fields and hills and forests.

A primeval echo repeated the loud shrill cry, the words "Mine! Mine! Mine!"—a fierce, courageous roar, and bright terrible laughter.

This laughter nearly doomed Cain. Because of it, Abel overpowered his brother, began to choke him, beat and crush him.

"Abel," said Cain. "There are two of us in the world. Once you kill me, what will you say to our father?"

Abel often thought of his father and mother, and now Cain unconsciously repeated the argument he didn't understand himself.

Abel let his brother go and left.

Cain lay on the ground by the forest. He closed his eyes, not from pain, but from grave thought, the first thought about the fate of humanity on earth.

Everything was quiet around him. The trees thought their own thoughts with wrinkled bark. The face of the earth was calm, majestic, and thoughtless. The bright shining sun indifferently illuminated the location of the first fraternal struggle.

5
ADAM IS BEHIND THE TIMES AND UNDERSTANDS NOTHING.

Adam looked upon the faces of his sons with calm, fatherly kindness. One face was covered in bruises and scrapes. Blood mixed with dirt in frozen brown clumps in the other's beard.

"What sort of beast attacked you, my children?" he asked.

"It was not an animal, but a man. My brother Cain attacked me," Abel lied.

Cain was silent.

"Why did he attack you?"

"It was because we split the world between us, and he wanted to claim what is mine for himself."

Adam understood nothing. Bewilderment streamed from his overgrown eyes.

"What does this mean, mine?"

Abel tried to explain it to him, but Adam still didn't understand anything. He rubbed his strong forehead with his dark broad palm.

"You're old, Father. You don't understand," Abel said irritably.

Adam left. He went into a faraway field, stepping heavily with his wide, thick, straightforward, and good-natured heels. A stubborn strange new thought pommeled at his head.

"Mine. What does that mean?"

The wind rustled in the grass, caressing his hair. The birds sang, a beast growled in the distance. The red sun shone at the edge of the field.

Adam looked at everything as though he saw it for the first time.

"Mine. What is mine? And what isn't?"

He walked to the vineyard and began to eat the thick, intoxicating fruit.

The grave new thought tormented him. He climbed a tree, sat on a branch. He stared. He thought. He accidentally fell asleep and fell off.

It was dark. The stars shone. The grass smelled of spices.

Adam scratched his head with firm fingers, rubbed the bruised spot. He returned to the hut and suddenly got into a fight with his sons. He shouted something incomprehensible and fiercely beat them with whatever was at hand. Eve screamed in a shrill voice. Cain fled into the forest. They finally calmed the old man down by morning.

6

AN INDISPUTABLE FACT: CAIN KILLED ABEL.

Cain slaughtered a ram, built a fire, and cooked himself supper. The dancing flame amused him, and he jumped around the fire and screamed. So as not to be disturbed, he settled down far from the family hut.

"Cain, why did you take and kill my ram?" asked Abel.

Cain went on jumping around the fire and amusing himself. But Abel wouldn't relent.

"Why did you take my ram?"

Cain suddenly grabbed the ram's carcass along with the stones it was laid upon, swung it mightily and hit his brother on the head.

"There's your ram," he shouted.

Two bodies—a dead ram and a man—merged for a moment into a one strange ugly whole and rolled together on the ground. The heavy flapping sound of a hit echoed through the forest, and a cloud of dust churned upward.

Cain left.

He worked all day. Worked even more willingly than usual, but before the sun set he dropped the stake he was using to aerate the field, and got to thinking. It seemed to him that his father asked, "Cain, where is your brother Abel?"

And he mentally replied: "Am I my brother's keeper?"

Instead of calming him down, the mental response troubled him. The first flash of human conscience was excruciating. He ran to the spot where they'd fought and stopped.

Abel and the dead ram lay equally unmoving in the dust.

A sharp pain gripped Cain's heart. For the first time ever, a human felt weak. Cain was the first person to need mental help, to need sympathy. He was the first to know loneliness.

But there was no sympathy even then. Mists fell solemnly over the ground, as though that was the most important thing. Clouds swirled in the sky. The sun rose and set solemnly. All kinds of grasses sprouted upward in their narrow existence, fat little pink worms writhed in the ground, the birds sang, the beasts roared, and everyone was infinitely busy with their own affairs. Nobody cared about human grief.

Cain went to the land of Nod, carrying on his broad shoulders the curse of a people not yet born and the slander of future generations.

Copyright © 1919 by Yefim Zozulya. Translation copyright © 2023 by Alex Shvartsman.

Marc A. Criley began writing in his early 50s, and his stories have since appeared in Beneath Ceaseless Skies, Abyss & Apex, Cossmass Infinities, *and elsewhere. Marc and his wife "manage" a household of cats in North Alabama, from where he blogs at kickin-the-darkness.com and 'Mastodons' as @MarcC@wandering.shop.*

THE GARDENER OF CERES

by Marc A. Criley

Jade, emerald, malachite. Kerwan, Dantu, Ialonus. Verdant crystals glowed across Ceres' cratered night-side disk. Hues of homecoming after four years away. The jadeite beads adorning Ezinu and Nawish drifted across the cabin window into Xenia's view. To the north, topaz and garnet pooled within Kaikara and Messor. *Oohs* and *ohmygods* and muffled profanities wafted through the cabin. Faces plastered against cool windows, cupped hands blocked dimmed lights. Seeing the gardens of Ceres for the first time through one's own eyes happened only once—usually. But it never got old.

Finally, Occator City, smack in the middle of the dark, salt-crusted crater; its ridges and valleys traced by luminous stems and curls of green and amber, of alfalfa fields, elm, oak, fig, teak, wheat, maize, quinoa, oats, rice. North and south, temperate forests. Patches of dull-red and gray deciduous woodlands neared the end of their autumn transition to winter dormancy. Ashlars of brown, emerald, and wheat. Patchwork dark fields under local night. From the last few kilometers above the spaceport the gardens stretched to the horizon.

"Everybody needs their greens," Xenia murmured as her bereft heart raced.

✧

After laying a palm on the customs sensor, *Xenia McMurdo, Serafina Interstellar Agricultural Consortium* and her photo flashed onto the display. The photo matched, mostly, what she saw each day in the mirror, though she'd cut the hair to a more accustomed bob. She was used to that face by now, though returning to Ceres underscored it was not the one she'd worn four years ago. She returned now only for heartbreak and an errand.

She'd already arranged for Mayvonne's frozen remains to be loaded onto the next shuttle, but going to the farm to retrieve the neuralscript could only be done in person. Then she'd head back out to Serafina, the asteroid-becoming-a-starship in its distant Jovian construction orbit, eighteen months later departing the solar system forever.

The customs booth chimed, the door slid aside. Xenia stepped through and traversed a short corridor to the Occator spaceport atrium, closed her eyes and inhaled the damp redolence of a greenhoused world. A half-dozen other passengers from the just-landed shuttle scooted through the modest terminal. Muscadine vines—*vitis rotundifolia*—draped the walls, rooted in concealed niches, screened away from direct light. Bougainvilleas, azaleas, *portulaca* filled raised beds. A massive fig tree, *ficus citrifolia*, dominated the space. Xenia slipped beneath its overarching limbs for one last sure moment of peace. The lowest branches, thick with leaves and fruit, arced twenty meters over her head, and in Ceres' low gravity the tree topped out somewhere over fifty. *The Cathedral of Figs* she'd christened it when she first arrived thirty years ago.

✧

A half-hour riding the Eastern Occator Spur line brought Xenia to the Carver Agricultural Station's transit depot. Just after five a.m. standard time; the local fields' pillar-mounted sunlights mimicked early morning twilight. Crickets murmured and katydids buzzed at their pre-dawn ebb. *Solar* dawn was still an hour or so away. The early shift farmers, botanists, entomologists, ecosynthesists, hydro engineers and soil pedologists with their dirt-caked fingernails would soon start arriving; heading to the fields and gardens, the pumping and debrining stations, farm sheds and ag labs.

Xenia spotted the self-serve transportation exchange, ordered up a gyro-stabilized moped. While the automation prepped it, she gazed off at the mist-shrouded field sector airlocks and diffuse forest of sunlight pillars. The thick scent of silverberry blooms tickled her nose, while humming bees swarmed over the flowers.

A cargo hauler skidded to a halt, almost clipping her. The furious driver jabbed a finger through the passenger window. "You've got a lot of nerve," he barked. "Mayvonne said you'd be back. I didn't believe it. Get back on that tram and get your ass off Ceres. Go back to that rock you stole!"

Nehsa.

Deep sideburns still plunged from his thick black hair, now shot through with silver threads. Xenia winced—*of course* his would be the first familiar face she'd see. Memories of that last Ceres Agricultural Steering Group weekend he hosted for the *gardeners* crashed into her head. Tables loaded with fresh produce, breads, pastas, fresh-clipped spices; the business and admin discussions; everyone sharing their latest departmental R&D projects; going over the latest reports from the Serafina Project's agriculture architects; breaking off for some VR and holo gaming; everyone wishing Mayvonne and Xenia well on their upcoming 'validate and verify' junket. Finally, by tradition, toasting out the weekend with the host's choice: an intense black raspberry vintage Nehsa fermented from his own brambles. Three bottles, the entire harvest, gone in one evening.

Right now his eyes burned wine-dark. "Go away."

"There's something I need to get from the residence," Xenia said. "And—"

"You're too late."

"I got the notice six weeks ago. I came as fast as I could."

Nehsa rolled his eyes. "Six weeks. Seriously. Mayvonne's been dead six weeks. I don't know what being an embodiment does to your brain, but I do know that paying one's respects to the dead consists of more than just claiming their frozen body."

Xenia's face froze. "Embodiments," she gritted, the nails of her clenched fists digging into her palms, "are human. Phylogenetically grown off the original. You *know* that. This body was grown and neuralscripted; it ages the same as you or any other original." Xenia glared at him. "Whether rejuvenative or curative, an embodiment is as human as you *and me*. I've known you for thirty years, Nehsa, I... I never took you for an *originalist*."

Nehsa looked chagrined. "That's not..." Then the anger returned. "Well I never took you for a dream-stealing thief and deserter. Turns out I'm a poor judge of character. You *abandoned* Mayvonne, left her to die alone. And what is this 'thirty' years business? I only knew you for ten before you deserted us."

Xenia looked away, red-faced, rubbed her forehead. "I meant.... That's not.... The orbital alignment was bad, Nehsa. Jupiter's at opposition, almost. Six weeks was the best I could do. I need to get out to the bottega, get to the residence, then we'll be gone. It'd be quicker with a ride."

Nehsa scoffed. "Hell no!"

"Sooner I get there, the sooner this'll be over."

"No."

"Nehsa, there's some—" She ducked as Nehsa amped the cargo hauler, its wheels spraying bits of loose gravel as he fishtailed out onto the farm road. Crates on the flatbed strained against their tie-downs. The whine of the hauler's electric drive subsided into the pre-dawn insect hum.

"Well, that went about as well as expected," Xenia muttered.

✡

When the blue, balloon-tired moped rolled up, Xenia threw her backpack into the cargo box, thumb-coded the lock, hopped on and shoved off. She pedaled and coasted twenty kilometers, passing through two farm sector airlocks as the morning sun pillars brightened. The Sena Reserve bottega had barely changed in the four years she'd been gone. Repainted, maybe. Modeled after a red-painted rural hay barn from the long ago midwestern US, it sported two open shed wings, one set up with picnic tables and food service stations, the other a shaded open classroom and presentation space. Two personal transports and a moped were parked out front. Her mouth watered at the smell of baking bread as she pedaled past it to the hardpan trail cutting through the grove of black locust, cedar, loblolly, and shumard oak. Leafcup, beautyberry, wild poinsettia, snakeroot, and myriad grasses and wildflowers carpeted a leaf-littered forest floor being ransacked by towhees, brown thrashers, and white-nosed fox squirrels. Minutes later the trail opened into a fifty meter wide clearing. A dark stained, rough-planed oak bungalow backed up against the brush line on the far side. *Home.*

Other than a new coat of paint and refreshed flowerbeds, the residence looked the same as when she'd left. She parked next to Nehsa's hauler, dropped the kickstand and slid off. Nehsa, sitting on the front porch steps, stood up. Alongside the sidewalk leading to the porch she passed the pressed metal and chipped enamel sign:

Mayvonne Cascadia
Gardener of Ceres Residence and Workshop
"Everybody needs their greens."

Xenia halted. Titmice, chickadees, and cardinals chirped and chattered in the surrounding woods. A wood thrush: upsong, pause, decrescendo.

"Nehsa…" she said.

"If you were going to show up and beg forgiveness," Nehsa growled, "you should've done it while she was still alive."

"It's complicated," Xenia murmured.

Nehsa rolled his eyes. "*Complicated*. Really. Why are you here?"

Xenia glanced up. "I got the notification that Mayvonne had passed." She paused. "Along with her private encryption key. I need to—"

"She got diagnosed with Cerean sulfurosis a month after she got back—after *you* kicked her off Serafina."

Xenia shook her head and tried to interrupt. "I didn't—"

"She was in a lot of pain before she died. Treatments helped a little. She kept working, went out to the fields up till six months ago. But you killed her, crushed her dreams. She was never the same after you dumped her." Nehsa took a step towards her. Xenia held her ground. "How could you do that?" he said. The hurt in his voice burned. "You two were…we thought you were going to get married when you got back!"

She grimaced, her heart aching. "Will you please let me speak?"

He didn't hear her, he was so shut off in his pain. "We were *all* a family—all us leads. You, Mayvonne, Besima, Big Yev, Emelda, me—all of us! We were making Ceres green *together*, and then…. And then you grabbed Serafina for yourself, and *just* for yourself. Pushed her away."

She shook her head in protest, but held her tongue. She knew now Nehsa needed to get this off his chest.

"What the *hell*, Xenia? You *knew* Mayvonne's dream was going to the stars! We thought you two would go *together*, do great things! We'd've said goodbye and wished you both a safe journey! The Gardens of Serafina!" He picked up a fistful of dirt, shook it in her face. "This is not yours. Not anymore. Get off our land. I can't even stand to look at you!" He threw the dirt down, spat, and strode towards the hauler. "You have no right to be here. Go away so we can forget we ever knew you."

Xenia took a deep breath. "Nehsa, *wait*," she implored. "Please—you need to listen to me." He slowed, but didn't stop. "Mayvonne's sulfurosis was diagnosed *on* Serafina." Nehsa halted. "Right then we knew we couldn't go—the disease was already too far along. But there was still a chance, something we both knew. Something *you* need to know. But you won't believe me if I just tell you, I have to show you. And I'm sorry but it's going to hurt you."

"Hurt me?" Nehsa said, speaking over his shoulder.

"Probably. Yes." Gesturing at the front door she said, "I need to get into the residence. Please?"

Nehsa swore under his breath, but reluctantly returned and led her up the steps.

✿

The porch door opened into a concrete-tiled mudroom, tidier now than it ever was when Xenia and Mayvonne lived there. A roller rack of overalls and jackets stood off to her right, a half-dozen pairs of boots lined up beneath. On the wall opposite the door the ivy-decorated peg rack held two work vests, pockets still stuffed with garden hand tools. *Her* work jacket, a bit more frayed than when she'd last seen it, hung on the leftmost peg, right where she'd left it when they'd departed for Serafina. Xenia opened the interior door and headed down the shotgun-style hallway. The walls had been repainted; nothing jarring, just lightened from hunter green to an elm-leaf shade. Braided twine tacked across each doorway blocked entry—first the big living room, then the kitchen, then the bathroom. The hallway cutting across the house to the side porch and workspace was open—she glanced down it to the side patio screen door. Next was Xenia's old office, now occupied with rack after rack of potted greenery.

At the next door she froze. The bedroom. Their bedroom. But stripped of every photo, holo, trinket, kitsch, doo-dad or freezer magnet that might remind one of Xenia, that might give away the truth.

Tears welled up, her shoulders slumped. All those years, all those memories discarded. A necessity, but necessity does little to ease one's pain. All for an uncertain, hoped-for future.

Xenia grabbed the twine braid and yanked the staple out of the wall.

"*What* are you doing?" Nehsa exclaimed. "You can't go— that's not for you, stop!" Xenia stepped into the bedroom.

Nehsa followed her in as she moved towards the closet. He reached out to grab her arm, hesitated. "Xenia!"

The closet door rattled as Xenia slid it aside. Tossing the backpack on the bed she dropped to her hands and knees, crawled halfway into the closet and dragged out a sturdy grey, featureless but for a hand-sized ID-plate, security box. Xenia settled back on her legs, looked up at the uncertainty and anger warring on Nehsa's face. "That's not yours!" he said.

"Yes it is." Xenia closed her eyes, dropped her chin, sighed. "Sorry. I'm just…it's…you need to see her. Just…just a couple more minutes."

"Her? Who? I don't understand," Nehsa said.

Xenia laid her left palm on the gray box's security plate. A soft click sounded as a dark seam appeared.

Nehsa leaned forward as Xenia raised the lid.

Reaching into the box, she felt around and drew out a pinky-sized metal cylinder embossed with an oak leaf. Tension washed away. Tears welled and slid down her cheeks. Grasping the cylinder in her fist, Xenia brought it to her lips and kissed it.

"That is…what?" Nehsa said. "An entanglement memory stick? That and Mayvonne's body are why you came back to Ceres?"

Xenia sat silent for a moment, grasping the cylinder, eyes closed. "It's not a memory stick," she breathed. She rose to her feet, shouldered the backpack. "We need to do this outside, there's not enough room in here."

He glared at her, ready to object, but turned and left the room, muttering. Xenia followed him down the hall, past the old office to the side passage. Emerging from the residence they both squinted as their eyes adjusted to the artificial sunlight of the Ceres morning. Not long now till the addition of solar dawn. The patio extended out about a dozen meters and ran the whole length of the residence, its hindmost third outfitted as a botanical prep area.

Raised garden beds heaped with fortified Cerean topsoil were packed with flowers and vegetables, a half-dozen tomato varieties, squash, and okra. Baskets of geraniums, pansies, and verbena hung from vine-wrapped pergolas. Hand-hewn oak stools and chairs were scattered around the patio, with a couple Adirondack-style chairs facing a low-walled firepit. A blue-striped skink fled into the surrounding grass.

"That firepit wasn't here before," Xenia said.

"Mayvonne was getting the chills," Nehsa said. "We put it in so she could have a fire when solar and standard night overlapped."

"Hmm," Xenia said.

"Said she liked to look at the stars, still hoped to see herself out there someday." Nehsa stuck a knife in: "But of course you made sure *that* wouldn't happen."

Xenia's sharp intake of breath startled Nehsa as she spun away and slammed a hand over her mouth, one wracking sob that wouldn't be stifled escaping.

Nehsa kept his suspicion-darkened eyes locked on her while she regained her composure. Settling herself, Xenia pulled a slim twenty centimeter square metal box out of the backpack, sat it on the patio and double-tapped its surface. A click sounded, followed by panels unfolding over and over, petaling out like a blooming flower. A pair of short audio-visual stalks and a control panel lined with circular and rectangular slots sprang up. Xenia swiped the panel, waited while the platform cycled through a rainbow sequence. A rotating, shapeshifting holographic test pattern appeared above it, quickly replaced by a green checkmark. A moment later the checkmark wavered, shimmered, and spiraled down into the base.

Xenia dropped to one knee, slid the cylinder she was holding into a slot. The projector sounded a flourish. Above it a woman abruptly appeared, lightly standing on the projector surface. Tall, strong arms, a long braided ponytail pulled forward over one shoulder, dressed in typical Ceres gardener gear—wearing a vest matching the *other* one hanging in the mudroom. Nehsa's jaw dropped.

In the stunned silence the figure spoke. "Dear Nehsa," she said, looking at him, "I know this has been hard. It was so unfair of us to do this to you." Her gaze flickered to her partner still kneeling on the ground. A hint of a smile appeared, then she turned back. "I'm so sorry we kept this a secret for so long."

"Xenia?" a perplexed Nehsa said, seeing a holographic Xenia as she looked four years ago.

The figure nodded, then squatted to face the woman Nehsa had wrongly believed to be her. "Mayvonne," she said, reaching to the edge of the holographic field until her fingertips flickered. "It is *so* good to see you home and alive. It is a balm for a hollowed heart."

"You're a...neuralscript AI, aren't you?" Nehsa sputtered at the holographic figure. He turned to the other. "And you're...I don't know what the hell you are. Or *who* you are..."

"*Not* an AI," Xenia said from the hologram projector, shaking her head as she stood up. "Fully realized neuralscript entity, but right now without my embodiment. Mayvonne's been wearing it for the last four years on Serafina."

"Mayvonne's *dead*," Nehsa hissed. "I was by her side here when she passed, heard her last breath. I made the memorial arrangements. *I* arranged to have her remains frozen, like she asked, instead of cremating them." He snarled directly at the person sitting on the patio. "I don't know what kind of sick thing you're pulling here, *Xenia*, but I will *not* stand for it. This is outrageous! God damn pathetic! This ends—"

"*Nehsa!*" The shout silenced Nehsa like a blow to the face as the woman shot from the ground and planted herself in front of him in a single low-grav stride. Her posture and tone were unmistakably pre-sulfurosis Mayvonne Cascadia, Gardener of Ceres. Her eyes burned into his. "*I. Was. Going. To. Die.* I knew it. Xenia knew it." She paused for a breath. "I know it is confusing to see me in Xenia's embodiment, wearing her face, but give me a moment to explain."

She stepped back and Nehsa looked back and forth between the hologram Xenia and Mayvonne-wearing-Xenia's-embodiment until he had them straight in his head. He nodded.

Mayvonne continued. "We'd finished our job on Serafina and were doing the neuralscript vetting required of everyone emigrating to Beta Hydri. Mine failed. They ran it again. It failed *again*. An exam turned up Cerean sulfurosis, which blocks the *substrate* neuralscripting. All they can pull is a *surface-level* emergent version of me and you can't reconstitute that into a phylogenetic embodiment, so I was done for. My original form was dying, and my scan was considered too incomplete to transfer with their rigid medical parameters I had failed to meet. In fact, I was going to *die* before Serafina ever left the solar system."

Nehsa gaped at her, shock and sadness reflected in his eyes.

"Xenia and I were *shattered*. We dreamed of going to the stars. The two of us. To bring what we grew here, what we *all* grew here, to another world, to transplant the roots of humanity out there. From Earth, to Ceres, to Serafina, to the stars. We dreamed of being together for as much of our lives as possible—sharing this journey, always. Then Xenia told me there was a way."

Xenia's holographic image crossed her arms. "I was embodied into a new form back when I was seventeen because my original body had incurable leukemia. So I know more than most *originals* about phylogenetic embodiment and neuralscripting." She took a simulated breath. "An emergent neuralscript, the shallow kind that can be read despite the sulfurosis plaques—*Mayvonne's* emergent neuralscript—can *overwrite* an *existing* neuralscript," she continued. "The embodiment's previous inhabitant—for want of a better term—had already stabilized the embodiment's neural matrix, so..."

Nehsa's eyes widened. He turned to Mayvonne in Xenia's form. "You didn't."

Mayvonne nodded. "I did. *We* did. We came up with a plan. I asked them to neuralscript me one more time; make a last ditch effort to know if it would work. We needed the most complete scan possible for our attempt. We told them to use whatever experimental settings or configurations they wanted to try. They were reluctant, but since I was the renowned *Gardener of Ceres* they humored me. *That* scan also failed, but it created an *emergent* neuralscript complete enough to be fully aware of what we were about to do."

"Then I..." Xenia paused, the hologram composing herself. "Then I scheduled a write refresh prophylactic scan of myself, and told them I wanted my neuralscript reverified to confirm no errors had developed over the years. I swapped Mayvonne's emergent-level neuralscript for mine. And then...I auto-okayed all mismatch overwrites to authorize the transfer."

"No," Nehsa objected. "That couldn't have happened! The techs would've known!"

Mayvonne shook her head, walking towards Xenia. "No, they wouldn't. Medical privacy, remember. What goes on in one's mind is...private." She reached the edge of the holographic field, reached into it. Fingers of flesh and ephemeral fingers of levitating nanoreflector intertwined and sparkled. "I have been without my heart too long."

Xenia sighed, while the projector rendered iridescent holographic tears. "On another world our hearts will *both* beat again."

☼

"Why didn't you tell us? *Me*." asked Nehsa, his eyes scrunched tight. "I was so angry. At Xenia...I thought. But now, I guess, it was you...Mayvonne. I'm now angry at *both* of you for letting us believe..." He rubbed his temples. "So this means that all along it had been Xenia's life in limbo. You allowed her to take this risk—to risk our entire existence on Cere. If the authorities had have believed any of the other gardners were involved..."

"You all would have been expelled from Cere. Yes, hence our deception." Mayvonne walked back to Nehsa, arms raised for an embrace, in entreaty. He retreated a step and defensively crossed his. She aborted, but laid a hand on his forearm—he didn't shake it off. "What we did was wildly illegal; it's considered homicide, killing Xenia, even *with* consent. Not to mention unethical. It wouldn't have mattered that it worked, that we could save Xenia in the form of a neuralscript holographic entity until she could be embodied again. It wouldn't have mattered that we can now *both* be reconstituted when Serafina reaches Beta Hydri. If anyone found out what we did, all hell would break loose."

Xenia took over. "We weren't just trying to just protect ourselves, but all the other gardeners. It was too risky to have two versions of Mayvonne in the same place, so one stayed and worked on Serafina while the other returned here. And we had to...discourage...questions. Hence making it seem like we had a massive falling out that 'Mayvonne' wouldn't—couldn't—talk about."

"You put all of us, *everyone*—Yev, Besima, everything—at risk," Nehsa repeated. "Just so you two could stay together."

"We did," Mayvonne admitted. "It was selfish. I didn't want to die, I..."

"But you *did!*" Nehsa protested. "You died. We *all* suffered through that. And then I had to freeze your body, rather than cremate it and spread the ashes here, where we..." He choked down a sob, whispered, "I *mourned* you." Then he turned to Xenia. "And I thought I had lost you, too, in a different way."

"I was here too, Nehsa," Xenia said quietly. Nehsa wiped his eyes. "While I lay dormant, most of the time—almost akin to being in a coma—there's a desktop neuralscript rig in Mayvonne's office. She spun me up so we could talk every couple of days, to tell me how she was doing, what everyone else was up to. How *you* were doing. Then I would go back into suspension..." She grimaced. "With each encounter, I watched the sulfurosis eat away at her. The *hardest thing* was her having to ask you to promise to freeze her remains after she passed—without telling you why."

"This embodiment," Mayvonne said, tapping her chest, "can now be *substrate* neuralscripted because there's no sulfurosis plaques in this form. Then it can be embodied into a phylogenetic off my original body when we arrive at Beta Hydri—that's why I needed to retrieve my body intact. Cerean sulfurosis isn't genetic, so it won't carry over. Then *this* embodiment can go back to its rightful owner." She smiled at Xenia.

"Nehsa," Xenia said, "I *know* how much you...and everyone, cared. Mayvonne saw your pain. Shared it with me..." She clasped her hands together, squeezed until their holographic rendition showed white. "I last saw her six days before she died." Her voice broke. "I—I couldn't be by her side, but I *was* in the room." Xenia wrapped her arms around herself. "I was here with both of you."

"I can't just forgive you. I—I need a moment to process this. You've had years," Nehsa pointed out. "But...I can understand why you did what you did. I would do anything for the one I loved, too.

Xenia nodded. "You were—*are*—Mayvonne's best and longest friend. She cared for you more than words can say. Keeping all this a secret has been tearing both versions of her apart, especially at the end."

Nehsa took a deep breath, let go an exhausted sigh. "She told me she was coming back." Tension and anger sloughed off his frame.

"What?" Mayvonne and Xenia exclaimed.

"A couple weeks before she died. We were sitting out here and had a little fire going in the pit. She spotted a shuttle dropping out of orbit, pointed it out to me and said, 'Xenia will be back for this old carcass after I'm gone, so don't let anything happen to it.' Then she laughed. 'I'll tell you everything when she gets here,' she said. I had no idea what that meant! I thought maybe it was the sulfurosis speaking." He looked at Mayvonne. "But now, here you are."

Mayvonne walked back over to Nehsa. He didn't retreat this time; she took one of his hands in both of hers. "Here I am. And I'm sorry it took so long, Nehsa. Xenia's known you for ten years. I've known you for almost thirty years now. You're a hell of a gardener and a hell of a friend. I'm glad that I was, in another life, able to spend my final hours with you."

Nehsa raised his other hand, hesitated, clasped Mayvonne's. The first shafts of true solar dawn filtered through the surrounding trees, glinted in Nehsa's shining eyes, illuminating a slow, reluctant smile.

"Thank you for loving her," Xenia said, clasping holographic hands over her heart.

Nehsa took a deep breath and released it. Anxiety, hope, and anticipation played across Xenia's holographic and Mayvonne's embodiment features. They'd come clean about the deception—at no small risk to themselves—to recover this friendship. Nehsa extended an olive branch. "I cooked up something new this season," he said. "Would you like to try some before you go?"

"What is it?"

"Ever had muscadine wine?"

Mayvonne shook her head. "No, but it sounds delicious."

"Mayvonne," Xenia called out, "don't think I didn't notice you cut my hair."

She blushed. "It'll grow out."

Copyright © 2023 by Marc A. Criley.

Mike Resnick, along with editing the first seven years of Galaxy's Edge *magazine, was the winner of five Hugos from a record thirty-seven nominations and was, according to* Locus, *the all-time leading award winner, living or dead, for short fiction. He was the author of over eighty novels, around 300 stories, three screenplays, and the editor of over forty anthologies. He was Guest of Honor at the 2012 Worldcon.*

OLD MACDONALD HAD A FARM

by Mike Resnick

I came to praise Caesar, not to bury him.

Hell, we all did.

The farm spread out before us, green and rolling, dotted with paddocks and water troughs. It looked like the kind of place you wish your parents had taken you when you were a kid and the world was still full of wonders.

Well, the world may not have been full of wonders any longer, but the farm was. Problem was, they weren't exactly the kind you used to dream of—unless you were coming down from a *really* bad acid trip.

The farm was the brainchild of Caesar Claudius MacDonald. He'd finally knuckled under to public pressure and agreed to show the place off to the press. That's where I came in.

My name's McNair. I used to have a first name, but I dumped it when I decided a one-word byline was more memorable. I work for the *SunTrib*, the biggest newstape in the Chicago area. I'd just broken the story that put Billy Cheever away after the cops had been after him for years. What I wanted for my efforts was my own syndicated column; what I got was a trip to the farm.

For a guy no one knew much about, one who almost never appeared in public, MacDonald had managed to make his name a household word in something less than two years. Even though one of his corporations owned our publishing company, we didn't have much on him in our files, just what all the other news bureaus had: he'd earned a couple of Ph. D.'s, he was a widower who by all accounts had been faithful to his wife, he'd inherited a bundle and then made a lot more on his own.

MacDonald was a Colorado native who emigrated to New Zealand's South Island, bought a 40,000-hectare farm, and hired a lot of technicians over the years. If anyone wondered why a huge South Island farm didn't have any sheep, they probably just figured he had worked out some kind of tax dodge.

Hell, that's what I thought too. I mean, why else would someone with his money bury himself on the underside of the globe for half a lifetime?

Then, a week after his 66th birthday, MacDonald made The Announcement. That's the year they had food riots in Calcutta and Rio and Manila, when the world was finding out that it was easier to produce eleven billion living human beings than to feed them.

Some people say he created a new life form. Some say he produced a hybrid (though not a single geneticist agrees with that.) Some—I used to snicker at them—say that he had delved into mysteries that Man Was Not Meant To Know.

According to the glowing little computer cube they handed out, MacDonald and his crew spent close to three decades manipulating DNA molecules in ways no one had ever thought of before. He did a lot of trial and error work with embryos, until he finally came up with the prototype he sought. Then he spent a few more years making certain that it would breed true. And finally he announced his triumph to the world.

Caesar MacDonald's masterpiece was the Butterball, a meat animal that matured at six months of age and could reproduce at eight months, with a four-week gestation period. It weighed 400 pounds at maturity, and every portion of its body could be consumed by Earth's starving masses, even the bones.

That in itself was a work of scientific brilliance—but to me the true stroke of genius was the astonishing efficiency of the Butterballs' digestive systems. An elephant, back when elephants still existed, would eat about 600 pounds of vegetation per day, but could only use about forty percent of it, and passed the rest as dung. Cattle and pigs, the most common meat animals prior to the Butterballs, were somewhat more efficient, but they, too, wasted a lot of expensive feed.

The Butterballs, on the other hand, utilized one hundred percent of what they were fed. Every pellet of food they ingested went right into building meat that was meticulously bio-engineered to please almost every palate. Anyway, that's what the endless series of P.R. releases said.

MacDonald had finally consented to allow a handful of pool reporters to come see for themselves.

We were hoping for a look at MacDonald too, maybe even an interview with the Great Man. But when we got there, we learned that he had been in seclusion for months. Turned out he was suffering from depression, which I would have thought would be the last thing to affect humanity's latest savior, but who knows what depresses a genius? Maybe, like Alexander, he wanted more worlds to conquer, or maybe he was sorry that Butterballs didn't weigh 800 pounds. Hell, maybe he had just worked too hard for too long, or maybe he realized that he was a lot closer to the end of life than the beginning and didn't like it much. Most likely, he just didn't consider us important enough to bother with.

Whatever the reason, we were greeted not by MacDonald himself, but by a flack named Judson Cotter. I figured he had to work in P.R.; his hair was a little too perfect, his suit too up-to-the-minute, his hands too soft for him to have been anything else but a pitchman.

After he apologized for MacDonald's absence, he launched into a worshipful biography of his boss, not deviating one iota from the holobio they'd shown us on the plane trip.

"But I suspect you're here to see the farm," he concluded after paraphrasing the bio for five minutes.

"No," muttered Julie Balch from *NyVid*, "we came all this way to stand in this cold wet breeze and admire your clothes."

A few of us laughed, and Cotter looked just a bit annoyed. I made a mental note to buy her a drink when the tour was done.

"Now let me see a show of hands," said Cotter. "Has anyone here ever seen a live Butterball?"

Where did they find you? I thought. *If we'd seen one, do you really think we'd have flown all the way to hell and gone just to see another?*

I looked around. No one had raised a hand. Which figured. To the best of my knowledge, nobody who didn't work for MacDonald had ever seen a Butterball in the flesh, and only a handful of photos and holos had made it out to the general public. There was even a rumor that all of MacDonald's employees had to sign a secrecy oath.

"There's a reason, of course," continued Cotter smoothly. "Until the international courts verified Mr. MacDonald's patent, there was always a chance that some unscrupulous individual or even a rogue nation would try to duplicate the Butterball. For that reason, while we have shipped and sold its meat all over the world, always with the inspection and approval of the local food and health authorities, we have not allowed anyone to see or examine the animals themselves. But now that the courts have ruled in our favor, we have opened our doors to the press." *Screaming bloody murder every step of the way,* I thought.

"You represent the first group of journalists to tour the farm, but there will be many more, and we will even allow Sir Richard Perigrine to make one of his holographic documentaries here at the farm." He paused. "We plan to open it to public tours in the next two or three years."

Suddenly a bunch of bullshit alarms began going off inside my head.

"Why not sooner, now that you've won your case?" asked Julie, who looked like she was hearing the same alarms.

"We'd rather that *you* bring the initial stories and holos of the Butterballs to the public," answered Cotter.

"That's very generous of you," she persisted. "But you still haven't told us why."

"We have our reasons," he said. "They will be made apparent to you before the tour is over."

My old friend Jake Monfried of the *SeattleDisk* sidled over to me. "I hope I can stay awake that long," he said sardonically. "It's all rubbish anyway."

"I know," I said. "Their rivals don't even need the damned holos. Any high school kid could take a hunk of Butterball steak and come up with a clone."

"So why haven't they?" asked Julie.

"Because MacDonald's got fifty lawyers on his payroll for every scientist," answered Jake. He paused, his expression troubled. "Still, this guy's lying to us—and it's a stupid lie, and he doesn't look *that* stupid. I wonder what the hell he's hiding?"

We were going to have to wait to find out, because Cotter began leading us across a rolling green plain toward a barn. We circled a couple of ponds, where a few dozen birds were wading and drinking. The whole setting looked like something out of a Norman Rockwell or a Grandma Moses painting, it was so wholesome and innocent—and yet every instinct I had screamed at me that something was wrong here, that nothing could be as peaceful and tranquil as it appeared.

"To appreciate what Mr. MacDonald has done here," said Cotter as we walked toward a large barn on a hillside, "you have to understand the challenge he faced. More than five billion men, women and children have serious protein deficiencies. Three billion of them are quite literally starving to death. And of course the price of meat—*any* meat—had skyrocketed to the point where only the very wealthy can afford it. So what he had to do was not only create an animal as totally, completely nutritious as the Butterball, he had to also create one that could mature and breed fast enough to meet mankind's needs now and in the future."

He stopped until a couple of laggards caught up with the group. "His initial work took the form of computer simulations. Then he hired a bevy of scientists and technicians who, guided by his genius, actually manipulated DNA to the point where the Butterballs existed not just on the screen and in Mr. MacDonald's mind, but in the flesh.

"It took a few generations for them to breed true, but fortunately a Butterball generation is considerably less than a year. Mr. MacDonald then had his staff spend some years mass-producing Butterballs. They were designed to have multiple births, not single offspring, and average ten to twelve per litter—and all of our specimens were bred and bred again so that when we finally introduced the Butterball to the world two years ago, we felt confident that we could keep up with the demand without running out of Butterballs."

"How many Butterballs have you got here?" asked the guy from *Eurocom International*, looking out across the rolling pastures and empty fields.

"We have more than two million at this facility," came the answer. "Mr. MacDonald owns some twenty-seven farms here and in Australia, each as large or larger than this one, and each devoted to the breeding of Butterballs. Every farm has its own processing plant. We're proud to note that while we have supplied food for billions, we've also created jobs for more than 80,000 men and women." He paused to make sure we had recorded that number or were jotting it down.

"That many?" mused Julie.

"I know it seems like we sneaked up on the world," said Cotter with a smile. "But for legal reasons we were compelled to keep the very existence of the Butterballs secret until we were ready to market them—and once we *did* go public, we were processing, shipping and selling hundreds of tons from each farm every month right from the start. We had to have all our people in place to do that."

"If they give him the Nobel, he can afford to turn the money down," Jake said wryly.

"I believe Mr. MacDonald is prepared to donate the money to charity should that happy event come to pass," responded Cotter. He turned and began walking toward the barn, then stopped about eighty feet from of it.

"I must prepare you for what you're going to—"

"We've already seen the holos," interrupted the French reporter.

Cotter stared at him for a moment, then began again. "As I was saying, I must prepare you for what you're going to *hear*."

"Hear?" I repeated, puzzled.

"It was a fluke," he explained, trying to look unconcerned and not quite pulling it off. "An accident. An anomaly. But the fact of the matter is that the Butterballs can articulate a few words, just as a parrot can. We could have eliminated that ability, of course, but that would have taken more experimentation and more time, and the world's hungry masses couldn't wait."

"So what do they say?" asked Julie.

Cotter smiled what I'm sure he thought was a comforting smile. "They simply repeat what they hear. There's no intelligence behind it. None of them has a vocabulary of more than a dozen words. Mostly they articulate their most basic needs."

He turned to the barn and nodded to a man who stood by the door. The man pushed a button, and the door slid back.

The first big surprise was the total silence that greeted us from within the barn. Then, as they heard us approaching—we weren't speaking, but coins jingle and feet scuff the ground—a voice, then a hundred, then a thousand, began calling out:

"Feed me!"

It was a cacophony of sound, not quite human, the words repeated again and again and again: *"Feed me!"*

We entered the barn, and finally got our first glimpse of the Butterballs. Just as in their holos, they were huge and roly-poly, almost laughably cute, looking more like oversized bright pink balloons than anything else. They had four tiny feet, good for balance but barely capable of locomotion. There were no necks to speak of, just a small pink balloon that swiveled atop the larger one. They had large round eyes with wide pupils, ears the size of small coins, two slits for nostrils, and generous mouths without any visible teeth.

"The eyes are the only part of the Butterball that aren't marketable," said Cotter, "and that is really for esthetic reasons. I'm told they are quite edible."

The nearest one walked to the edge of its stall.

"Pet me!" it squeaked.

Cotter reached in and rubbed its forehead, and it squealed in delight.

"I'll give you a few minutes to wander around the barn, and then I'll meet you outside, where I'll answer your questions."

He had a point. With a couple of thousand Butterballs screaming *"Feed me!"* more and more frantically, it was almost impossible to think in there. We went up and down the rows of small stalls, captured the place on film and tape and disk and cube, then went back outside.

"That was impressive," I admitted when we'd all gathered around Cotter again. "But I didn't see any two million Butterballs in there. Where are the rest of them?"

"There are more than three hundred barns and other enclosures on the farm," answered Cotter. "Furthermore, close to half a million are outside in pastures."

"I don't see anything but empty fields," remarked Jake, waving a hand toward the pristine enclosures.

"We're a huge farm, and we prefer to keep the Butterballs away from prying eyes. In fact, this barn was built only a month ago, when we finally decided to allow visitors on the premises. It is the only building that's as close as a mile to any of our boundary lines."

"You said that some of them were in pastures," said Julie. "What do they eat?"

"Not grass," answered Cotter. "They're only outside because they're multiplying so fast that we're actually short of barns at the moment." He paused. "If you looked carefully at them, you noticed that grazing is quite beyond their capabilities." He held up a small golden pellet for us to see. "This is what they eat. It is totally artificial, created entirely from chemicals. Mr. MacDonald was adamant that no Butterball should ever eat any product that might nourish a human being. Their digestive systems were engineered to utilize this particular feed, which can provide nourishment to no other species on Earth."

"As long as you tinkered with their digestive systems, why didn't you make them shit-eaters?" asked Jake, only half-jokingly. "They could have served two purposes at once."

"I assume that was meant in jest," said Cotter, "but in point of fact, Mr. MacDonald considered it at one time. After all, some nourishment *does* remain in excrement—but alas, not enough. He wanted an animal that could utilize one hundred percent of what we fed it."

"How smart are they?" asked one of the Brits. "When I was a child, I had a dog that always wanted me to feed it or pet it, but it never told me so."

"Yes it did," said Cotter. "It just didn't use words."

"Point taken," said the Brit. "But I'd still like to know…"

"These are dumb farm animals," said Cotter. "They do not think, they do not dream, they have no hopes or aspirations, they do not wish to become Archbishop. They just happen to be able to articulate a few words, not unlike many birds. Surely you don't think Mr. MacDonald would create a sentient meat animal."

"No, of course not," interjected Julie. "But hearing them speak is still a bit of a shock."

"I know," said Cotter. "And that's the *real* reason we've invited you here, why we're inviting so many other press pools—to prepare the public."

"That's going to take a lot of preparation," I said dubiously.

"We have to start somewhere," said Cotter. "We have to let the people know about this particular anomaly. Men love to anthropomorphize, and a talking animal makes doing so that much easier. The consumers must be made to understand, beyond any shadow of a doubt, that these are unintelligent meat animals, that they do not know what their words mean, that they have no names and aren't pets, that they do not mourn the loss of their neighbors any more than a cow or a goat does. They are humanity's last chance—note that I did not even say humanity's last *best* chance—and we cannot let the protestors and picketers we know will demonstrate against us go unanswered. No one will believe *our* answers, but they should believe the answers of the unbiased world press."

"Yeah," I said under my breath to Jake. "And if kids didn't want to eat Bambi, or Henry the Turkey, or Penelope Pig, how is anyone going to make them dig into Talky the Butterball, who actually exists?"

"I heard that," said Cotter sharply, "and I must point out that the children who will survive because of the Butterballs will almost certainly never have been exposed to Bambi or Henry or any of the others."

"Maybe not for a year or two," I replied, unimpressed. "But before long you'll be selling Butterburgers on every street corner in the States."

"Not until we've fulfilled our mission among the less fortunate peoples of the world—and by that time the people you refer to should be prepared to accept the Butterballs."

"Well, you can hope," I said.

"If it never comes to that, it doesn't really matter," said Cotter with an elaborate shrug. "Our mission is to feed Earth's undernourished billions."

We both knew it would come to that, and sooner than anyone planned, but if he didn't want to argue it, that was fine with me. I was just here to collect a story.

"Before I show you the processing plant, are there any further questions?" asked Cotter.

"You mean the slaughterhouse, right?" said Jake.

"I mean the processing plant," said Cotter severely. "Certain words are not in our lexicon."

"You're actually going to show us Butterballs being … *processed*?" asked Julie distastefully.

"Certainly not," answered Cotter. "I'm just going to show you the plant. The process is painless and efficient, but I see no value in your being able to report that you watched our animals being prepared for market."

"Good!" said Julie with obvious relief.

Cotter gestured to an open bus that was parked a few hundred meters away, and it soon pulled up. After everybody was seated, he climbed on and stood next to the driver, facing us.

"The plant is about five miles away, at almost the exact center of the farm, insulated from curious eyes and ears."

"Ears?" Julie jumped on the word. "Do they scream?"

Cotter smiled. "No, that was just an expression. We are quite humane, far more so than any meat packing plant that existed before us."

The bus hit a couple of bumps that almost sent him flying, but he hung on like a trooper and continued bombarding us with information, about three-quarters of it too technical or too self-serving to be of any use.

"Here we are," he announced as the bus came to a stop in front of the processing plant, which dwarfed the barn we had just left. "Everyone out, please."

We got off the bus. I sniffed the air for the odor of fresh blood, not that I knew what it smelled like, but of course I couldn't detect any. No blood, no rotting flesh, nothing but clean, fresh air. I was almost disappointed.

There were a number of small pens nearby, each holding perhaps a dozen Butterballs.

"You have perhaps noticed that we have no vehicles capable of moving the hundreds and thousands of units we have to process each day?" asked Cotter, though it came out more as a statement than a question.

"I assume they are elsewhere," said the lady from India.

"They were inefficient," replied Cotter. "We got rid of them."

"Then how do you move the Butterballs?"

Cotter smiled. "Why clutter all our roads with vehicles when they aren't necessary?" he said, tapping out a design on his pocket computer. The main door to the processing plant slid open, and I noticed that the Butterballs were literally jumping up and down with excitement.

Cotter walked over to the nearest pen. "Who wants to go to heaven?" he asked.

"Go to heaven!" squeaked a Butterball.

"Go to heaven!" rasped another.

Soon all twelve were repeating it almost as if it were a chant, and I suddenly felt like I was trapped inside some strange surrealistic play.

Finally Cotter unlocked their pen and they hopped—I hadn't seen any locomote at the other barn—up to the door and into the plant.

"It's as simple as that," said Cotter. "The money we save on vehicles, fuel and maintenance allows us to—"

"There's nothing simple about it!" snapped Julie. "This is somewhere between blasphemy and obscenity! And while we're at it," she added suspiciously, "how can a dumb animal possibly know what heaven is?"

"I repeat, they are not sentient," said Cotter. "Just as you have code words for your pet dog or cat, we have them for the Butterballs. Ask your dog if he wants a treat, and he'll bark or sit up or do whatever you have conditioned him to do. We have conditioned the Butterballs in precisely the same way. They don't know the meaning of the word 'heaven' any more than your pet knows the meaning of the word 'treat,' but we've conditioned them to associate the word with good feelings and with entry into the processing plant. They will happily march miles through a driving rain to 'go to heaven.'"

"But heaven is such a ... a *philosophical* concept," persisted the Indian woman. "Even to use it seems—"

"Your dog knows when he's been good," interrupted Cotter, "because you tell him so, and he believes you implicitly. And he knows when he's been bad, because you show him what he's done to displease you and you call him a bad dog. But do you think he understands the abstract philosophical concepts of good and bad?"

"All right," said Julie. "You've made your point. But if you don't mind, I'd rather not see the inside of the slaughterhouse."

"The processing plant," he corrected her. "And of course you don't have to enter it if it will make you uncomfortable."

"I'll stay out here too," I said. "I've seen enough killing down in Paraguay and Uruguay."

"We're not killing anything," explained Cotter irritably. "I am simply showing you—"

"I'll stay here anyway," I cut him off.

He shrugged. "As you wish."

"If you have no vehicles to bring them to the plant," asked the Brit, approaching the entrance, "how do you move the … uh, the finished product out?"

"Through a very efficient system of underground conveyers," said Cotter. "The meat is stored in subterranean freezers near the perimeter of the property until it is shipped. And now…" He opened a second pen, offered them heaven, and got pretty much the same response.

Poor bastards, I thought as I watched them hop and waddle to the door of the plant. *In times gone by, sheep would be enticed into the slaughterhouse by a trained ram that they blindly followed. But leave it to us to come up with an even better reward for happily walking up to the butcher block: heaven itself.*

The Butterballs followed the first dozen into the belly of the building, and the rest of the pool followed Cotter in much the same way. There was a parallel to be drawn there, but I wasn't interested enough to draw it.

I saw Julie walking toward one of the pens. She looked like she didn't want any company, so I headed off for a pen in the opposite direction. When I got there, four or five of the Butterballs pressed up against the fence next to me.

"Feed me!"

"Feed me!"

"Pet me!"

"Feed me!"

Since I didn't have any food, I settled for petting the one who was more interested in being petted than being fed.

"Feel good?" I asked idly.

"Feel good!" it said.

I almost did a double-take at that.

"You're a hell of a mimic, you know that?" I said.

No reply.

"Can you say what I say?" I asked.

Silence.

"Then how the hell did you learn to say it feels good, if you didn't learn it just now from me?"

"Pet me!"

"Okay, okay," I said, scratching it behind a tiny ear.

"Very good!"

I pulled my hand back as if I'd had an electric shock. "I never said the word 'very.' Where did you learn it?" *And more to the point, how did you learn to partner it with 'good'?*

Silence.

For the next ten minutes I tried to get it to say something different. I wasn't sure what I was reaching for, but the best I got was a *"Pet me!"* and a pair of *"Goods"*.

"All right," I said at last. "I give up. Go play with your friends, and don't go to heaven too soon."

"Go to heaven!" it said, hopping up and down. *"Go to heaven!"*

"Don't get so excited," I said. "It's not what it's cracked up to be."

"See Mama!" it squealed.

"What?"

"See God! See Mama!"

Suddenly I knew why MacDonald was being treated for depression. I didn't blame him at all.

I hurried back to the slaughterhouse, and when Cotter emerged alone a moment later I walked up to him.

"We have to talk," I said, grabbing him by the arm.

"Your colleagues are all inside inspecting the premises," he said, trying to pull himself loose from my grip. "Are you sure you wouldn't care to join them?"

"Shut up and listen to me!" I said. "I just had a talk with one of your Butterballs."

"He told you to feed him?"

"He told me that he would see God when he went to heaven."

Cotter swallowed hard. "Oh, shit—another one!"

"Another one of *what?*" I demanded. "Another sentient one?"

"No, of course not," said Cotter. "But as often as we impress the need for absolute silence among our staff, they continue to speak to each other in front of the Butterballs, or even to the Butterballs themselves. Obviously this one heard someone saying that God lives in heaven. It has no concept of God, of course; it probably thinks God is something good to eat."

"He thinks he's going to see his mother, too," I said.

"He's a *mimic!*" said Cotter severely. "Surely you don't think he can have any memory of his mother? For Christ's sake, he was weaned at five weeks!"

"I'm just telling you what he said," I replied. "Like it or not, you've got a hell of a P.R. problem: Just how many people do you want him saying it to?"

"Point him out to me," said Cotter, looking panicky. "We'll process him at once."

"You think he's the only one with a vocabulary?" I asked.

"One of the very few, I'm sure," said Cotter.

"Don't be *that* sure," said Julie, who had joined us while I was talking to Cotter. She had an odd expression on her face, like someone who's just undergone a religious experience and wishes she hadn't. "Mine looked at me with those soft brown eyes and asked me, very gently and very shyly, not to eat it."

I thought Cotter's would shit in his expensive suit. "That's impossible!"

"The hell it is," she shot back.

"They are *not* sentient," he said stubbornly. "They are *mimics*. They do not think. They do not know what they are saying." He stared at her. "Are you sure he didn't say *'feed'*? It sounds a lot like *'eat.'* You've got to be mistaken."

It made sense. I hoped he was right.

"'Don't feed me?'" repeated Julie. "The only unhungry Butterball on the farm?"

"Some of them speak better than others. He could have been clearing his throat, or trying to say something that came out wrong. I've even come across one that stutters." It occurred to me that Cotter was trying as hard to convince himself as he was to convince her. "We've tested them a hundred different ways. They're not sentient. They're *not!*"

"But—"

"Consider the facts," said Cotter. "I've explained that the words sounds alike. I've explained that the Butterballs are not all equally skilled at articulation. I've explained that after endless lab experiments the top animal behavioral scientists in the world have concluded that they are not sentient. All that is on one side. On the other is that you *think* you may have heard something that is so impossible that any other explanation makes more sense."

"I don't know," she hedged. "It sounded exactly like…"

"I'm sure it did," said Cotter soothingly. "You were simply mistaken."

"No one else has ever heard anything like that?" she asked.

"No one. But if you'd like to point out which of them said it…"

She turned toward the pen. "They all look alike."

I tagged along as the two of them walked over to the Butterballs. We spent about five minutes there, but none of them said anything but *"Feed me!"* and *"Pet me!"*, and finally Julie sighed in resignation.

"All right," she said wearily. "Maybe I was wrong."

"What do you think, Mr. McNair?" asked Cotter.

My first thought was: what the hell are you asking *me* for? Then I looked into his eyes, which were almost laying out the terms of our agreement, and I knew.

"Now that I've had a few minutes to think about it, I guess we were mistaken," I said. "Your scientists know a lot more about it than we do."

I turned to see Julie's reaction.

"Yeah," she said at last. "I suppose so." She looked at the Butterballs. "Besides, MacDonald may be a zillionaire and a recluse, but I don't think he's a monster, and only a monster could do something like … well … yes, I must have been mistaken."

And that's the story. We were not only the first pool of journalists to visit the farm. We were also the last.

The others didn't know what had happened, and of course Cotter wasn't about to tell them. They reported what they saw, told the world that its prayers were answered, and only three of them even mentioned the Butterballs' special talent.

I thought about the Butterballs all during the long flight home. Every expert said they weren't sentient, that they were just mimics. And I suppose my Butterball could very well have heard someone say that God lived in heaven, just as he could have heard someone use the word "very." It was a stretch, but I could buy it if I had to.

But where did Julie Balch's Butterball ever hear a man begging not to be eaten? I've been trying to come up with an answer to that since I left the farm. I haven't got one yet—but I *do* have a syndicated column, courtesy of the conglomerate that owns the publishing company.

So am I going use it to tell the world?

That's my other problem: Tell it *what?* That three billion kids can go back to starving to death? Because whether Cotter was telling the truth or lying through his teeth, if it comes down to a choice between Butterballs and humans, I know which side I have to come down on.

There are things I can control and things I can't, things I know and things I am trying my damnedest not to know. I'm just one man, and I'm not responsible for saving the world.

But I *am* responsible for me—and from the day I left the farm, I've been a vegetarian. It's a small step, but you've got to start somewhere.

Copyright © 2001 by Mike Resnick. First appeared in Asimov's, September 2001.

Alan Smale is the double Sidewise Award-winning author of the Clash of Eagles trilogy, and his shorter fiction has appeared in Asimov's *and numerous other magazines and original anthologies. His latest novel,* Hot Moon, *came out last year from CAEZIK SF & Fantasy. When he is not busy creating wonderful new stories, he works as an astrophysicist and data archive manager at NASA's Goddard Space Flight Center.*

LEAP OF FAITH

by Alan Smale

Levi traipsed into the city of Shadom footsore and blistered, crusted with the salt of his own sweat. A deep scratch along his right thigh from groin to knee was his only serious wound, yet it ached and stung like the very Devil, and his shoulders ached from leaning part of his weight on his wooden staff. Having survived the Vasty Deeps by the skin of his teeth, Levi badly needed to rest and heal. His youthful God had other ideas.

Time and space stabilized once he passed through the giant arched gates. No longer did the city look blue to him; no longer did the mountains appear reddened when he glanced back. Everything was now a washed-out desert tan, and Levi in his exhaustion felt the same color.

His face was warm but the back of his neck felt chilled. Ignoring the sneers of the gate-guards, who doubtless took him for one of the crazy desert prophets, Levi knelt and kissed the dirt, giving thanks to God for his successful return.

As he did so the full stream of his earthly Shadom memories returned, hitting him between the eyes like a boulder. He stood and nodded. He now knew his way home.

A woman beating the dust out of a rug looked up as Levi passed, and gestured to avert the Evil Eye. Levi did, after all, look as if he had been excreted from the bowels of Hell.

He glanced left and right into other people's homes as he walked by. Here lived the ordinary folk, men and women who ate and worked, farmed and traded, cared for one another and raised children.

Their real lives had continued and progressed in Levi's absence, and he obscurely envied them their normality. How different would the world be, once it was fully formed? Once God's Creation was finished, could Levi return permanently to a life here in Shadom? And what would that be like?

Or would there always be more to do, out in the bright and the dark?

Entering the city square, Levi passed by the Tower of Clockwork. Even as the spirals and murals on the Tower walls dazzled him, he noted the clock still held its time adequately against the more accurate giant sundial in the center of the square. In the mountains, and above the Earth, Levi's days had moved at a variable pace, stretching interminably or ending without warning, the land rocking under his feet. Bushes would burn. Snakes would occasionally clear their throats and speak, to offer him wealth incalculable. Such distractions he had ignored, knowing them to be only echoes of the true salvation that was to be found through God.

And in the Deeps, of course, he hadn't been able to see the sun at all.

The back of his neck tingled. A shout of warning pierced his reverie. He looked up in time to see Lilith swoop down out of the air, serpentine and majestic, all black hair and snarl. She plunged into the streets, jaws wide. But the city was ready for her, as always. On the housetops and Tower, bowmen stepped out of cover: uniformed Justicemen, city guards, even some of the Crass-men in their rags, all briefly united in a single goal. Lilith roared by Levi at speed—with a literal roar—not thirty feet above him, as the bows bent and the arrows flew.

Riddled with arrows, the demon plummeted to the sand and exploded into smoke and fleshy wreckage that quickly burned and evaporated, leaving naught behind. A half-hearted cheering broke out, quickly silenced. It was too hot to get excited. Especially since tomorrow Lilith would reappear in the skies and attack Shadom once more, and again the day after, until they could figure out a better way of dealing with her.

Sometimes Lilith did get past their defenses. Sometimes she smashed buildings, even killed and maimed.

Next to the Tower of Clockwork was a wellhead. Levi unbuckled his cloak, stripped to the waist and pumped the handle, allowing the water to sluice the desert grime from him. He soon stood in a growing puddle of his own filth, yet the water rejuvenated him as if it had flowed directly into his blood. From the other side of the square a jezebel watched him, a water-jug on her head and her hand on her hip, tongue darting along her lips, no doubt wondering whether he had any money.

Levi carried none, and was God's man and a family man besides.

He brushed the drops from his skin and was preparing to go home when the angels walked into the city square.

They were so similar to each other that they might have been the same being, duplicated. Almost impossibly beautiful, their features were as delicate as glazed pots. Their skin was a blueish-white where Levi's was olive, their chins smooth and unblemished. Levi had never actually seen an angel before, as far as he recalled, but their provenance was clear. The jezebel gaped at them, fear and lust warring on her features.

The angels headed straight for Levi. "Sanctuary," said the leftmost, and "Hospitality", the one on the right.

Levi sighed. This could mean nothing but trouble.

✡

And yet, a degree of caution was in order. The snakes that tried to tempt him in the mountains had fine glossy skins, too. "You know me?" he said cautiously.

"You are Levi." "A good man." "Wise and conscientious." "Servant of the Lord." "His mark is upon you." "More of a glow, really."

As if they were a single being with two bodies and two mouths. Levi studied them with professional interest. "We've met before?"

"No." "But we have always known you."

He shook his head, bemused. "Who are you?"

"Visitors." "From another place."

"Another…?"

"We must be circumspect," said one, apologetically.

Indeed, the angels had already drawn an unhealthy degree of attention. Like moths to a flame, Crass-men were ambling into the square. Interest was growing. The jezebel was touching herself coarsely, unable to resist; beneath the odd blue shifts the angels wore, their forms were just too perfect.

And where there was no lust, there was fear. A small boy ran up and pitched a well-aimed stone. The leftmost angel watched its arc through the air with detached interest, and then said "Ow," as it bounced off his shoulder.

Like it or not, the angels were under Levi's protection.

"Come with me," he said.

✡

His little Leah threw herself on him with a squeal, wrapping her arms around his thighs. He lifted his daughter and tossed her lightly in the air, laughing.

Rebekah, his wife, stopped her bread-making long enough to say darkly, "So, deigning to pay us a visit? The Lord run out of rocks for you to move?" She went back to pounding the dough with renewed vigor. Levi went and kissed her cheek anyway, and Rebekah bore it with grudging grace.

Deborah did not rise from her stool in the corner of the room, but eyed him suspiciously from beneath her hair. Levi's eldest daughter had been just entering puberty when Levi had left for the mountains, and clearly she'd sprinted through it in his absence. He did not attempt to hug her. "Were you bad?" he said, attempting jocularity. "Made to sit in the corner?"

"I sit where I please," she said sullenly.

"Excellent," said Levi under his breath, and then the angels walked in behind him.

His family's reaction to their entrance was much more dramatic. Rebekah gasped and dropped her mixing bowl. Dough spattered on her feet. Leah, immensely startled, toppled backward like a much younger child and sat down on the floor with a bump. Deborah's intake of breath was almost a hiss; her face turned bright red as she eyed the strangers up and down almost as wantonly as the jezebel. "Arms," said Levi, and as vacantly as a golem Deborah pulled a shawl over her bare shoulders for propriety.

Perhaps Levi should have warned them, but a man had to take his entertainment where he could.

It seemed the angels had been born in a barn. Levi walked behind them to close the door, glancing into the street as he did so. About a dozen people had followed them home; urchins, jezebels, and Crass-men. Now might have been an apropos time for Lilith to have swooped and snatched a few, breathing fire, but Levi did not sense the demon anywhere near. He closed the door firmly.

"Dad?" said Deborah, coming up close beside him.

"It's good to see you all," said Levi to his family. "I acquitted myself well in the Deeps, as best I remember. I was true and faithful to the Lord. And as you see, we have guests."

"From the *Deeps*?" said Rebekah.

Levi turned to the angels politely. With their strange double-act prose, they spoke in Levi's house for the first time. "Not the Deeps." "We are from beyond." "We thank you, Levi." "And we extend our gratitude to your family for their hospitality."

"This is my wife, Rebekah," said Levi. "My daughters, Deborah and Leah. And you are…?"

"We fell here," said one as if it explained everything, and the other added, "We have no names."

"No names?" said Deborah. "Great. Nothing odd about *that*."

"They're guests, Deborah," Levi said mildly. "Show courtesy."

His wife came forward with a bowl of water to wash their guests' feet, as was the custom, but her hands shook so hard that she slopped the water as she knelt.

The angels stepped away delicately. "Please." "That is not necessary." Nor was it; their bare feet were smooth and bore not even the merest specks of dust. Her eyes lingering, Rebekah gave a tiny groan.

Clearly Levi needed to assert some control. "Perhaps you would like to rest from your long, uh, downward journey," he said to the nameless ones, rather pointedly.

"We do not rest," they said, whereupon—without even a glance at Levi—Deborah picked up the ball and responded with unimpeachable courtesy, "Then, we beseech you, allow us a few brief moments as a family to prepare you a fitting repast," and guided them through the curtain into the back area of the house, where the sleeping and ablutions rooms were.

As she came immediately back, Rebekah said "Deborah, that was rude and—"

"—and well done," said Levi.

"Well done?" Rebekah looked horrified. "Addressing such beings with such familiarity?"

"*I'm* not the one on my knees," Deborah pointed out coolly, and went to pick up her sister.

"I'm scared of them," said Leah. "What do they want with us?"

Which was exactly the right question. But Levi had no answer. "How are you all? Are you well?"

"Well enough," muttered Rebekah, back on her feet now and opening and closing baskets to see what food she had in the house.

"Deborah's had a boyfriend," said Leah, rather gleefully.

"Hush, brat," said Deborah. "But if I have, I'm not the only one."

"What?" Leah, outraged, jabbed her older sister in the stomach. "Not I, not hardly, not boys, blech!" and made a face as if she was chewing dirt, but Levi, one step ahead, glanced over to where Rebekah labored over the meal with averted eyes.

"Leah, help your mother. Deborah, I need to talk to you."

"Boys like to look at me!" Deborah cried. "I've done nothing wrong! It's all just gossip and … slander!"

"And you swear that?"

She met his eye defiantly. "Do I need to?"

"Leah, didn't I tell you to help your mother? Deborah, didn't I ask to speak to you alone? *Now*, please."

From dealing with Deborah as a child, Levi knew she was about to explode. He gave her a solemn wink and shook his head slightly, and the stinging words died on her lips. She looked at him quizzically, then shrugged and stalked from the room.

"I'll deal with this," he said to his wife.

"Of course," Rebekah said sarcastically. "Just as you always have. She's impossible, Levi. The time for you to be a *father* was six months ago, or six years. You can't just *appear*."

Levi thought of the angels again, since that was exactly what they'd done. "No, I'm sure you're right."

Deborah waited just outside the front door, staring at the small crowd who stood in the shade across the road. "Those frigging angels are going to be trouble for us," she said.

"Language." Levi took her arm and ushered her around the corner of the house, out of sight of the growing mob. "Are you all right?"

"What, me? Of course. What about *you*?"

"Yes."

Despite her familiarity, despite the easy way they'd worked the situation with Rebekah and the angels, Levi found himself alone with someone he hardly knew. "How long was I away?"

"Seven months," she said resentfully. "And eighteen days. Not that *I* was the one counting."

Far more than the forty days and nights he had expected, then. This was not spring, but autumn. Levi tried to keep the shock from registering on his face. He should have guessed, he now realized; from the change in Deborah, from the length of Leah's hair, the depth of Rebekah's animosity, even the position of the sun in the sky. Any one of a dozen clues.

The Lord's demands on him were heavy.

"Well," he said at last. "I've missed a lot, then."

She shrugged, and he remembered his excuse for calling her out here in the first place. "And you've had a man?"

She looked at him.

"Deborah. It's just me. Nobody else has to know."

She laughed. "Everyone else thinks they know already."

"So?"

"Not a *man*. A boy. And I was careful. I'm not with child. I was just playing. I just wanted to know how it all *worked*, Dad."

Despite his half-horror, Levi laughed. "Yes. *You*? Of course you did. But, Deborah—"

"I need to show you something," she said, and pulled him toward a lean-to against the side of the house, a small shack he didn't recognize, barely anything, perhaps a hut for tools. She did a complicated thing to its door handle that he didn't catch, and opened the door.

He didn't know what he'd expected, but certainly not this.

Tools, yes, and a second door that must lead into the house. But also a strange object: two flat circles of wood, joined with straight, sturdy bars. She lifted it and pushed at the rear wheel, which spun with a clicking sound.

Levi had just spent forty days—no, seven *months*—driving the giant machines of the Lord, but the memories of that had faded. Deborah's contraption confounded him. "What is it?"

"This is my third attempt. Mother made me burn the first two, and then we came to, well, an agreement.

But this version is better anyway. See how easily?" She spun the wheel again. "And the lever here, look."

"Yes?"

"I was at the Clockwork Tower, winding the mechanism as you taught me." Levi suffered another split-minded moment. Had he taught Deborah to do that? Obviously so. "And, looking at those *cogs*, I thought of this."

As a cart it could never balance, and the load it would bear on its cross-beam would be small. Yet to the other half of Levi's brain, the now-hidden half, it seemed important. "You're going to have to tell me, Deborah."

His obtuseness startled her. She touched his forehead, miming scorn, as if he had a fever that befuddled him; a jokey gesture from her long-ago childhood. "It carries a person, Dad. You ride it as you'd ride a camel or an ass, with one leg on each side. Stand astride it and push till the wheels roll, then rocking this hand-lever applies more strength to propel you forward than you can apply directly with your legs. Faster than walking or even running, yet—"

"You've ridden *astride* this thing?" Levi backed away from his daughter's invention as if it were a snake. Wild images of her shame flooded his mind. No wonder Deborah was slandered, no wonder her reputation had grown so base and contemptible…."

Deborah put her hand on her hip, reminding him fleetingly of the jezebel. Her hair fell over her eyes. "Dad. Really? I just told you I played with a boy, and you're all hot and bothered about me putting my leg over *this*?"

"Well," said Levi. "*This* you did in public."

Then the hidden portion of his brain caught up. "But, yes, it's very clever."

She had designed and built this all by herself. Deborah had never seen the engines of God's creation. She had not been above and beneath the world as Levi had; his daughter's skills were born of her own intelligence, her own gifts and efforts.

And the twin-wheeled conveyance was truly remarkable. Especially the lever, so that legs and one hand could all assist in powering it, while the second hand steered. How fast might someone travel on such a thing?

"I'm very proud of you," he muttered.

"Pardon?"

Levi forced himself to focus. They didn't have time for this. Trouble was coming that he did not know how to avert. "Deborah, I need you to help me. With the angels."

"Yes," she said coolly, and Levi realized she had been expecting this.

"I need your opinion. I can't trust my own perceptions. Are they truly from God? Do you trust them? Tell me what you *really* think, Deborah, not what I might prefer to hear."

"Dad, I've seen them for all of thirty seconds."

"Later. Tonight. Just help me."

"All right." She mulled it over. "I can speak my mind to them, then? Ask them questions? I have your permission?"

"Be careful. But, yes."

"Then you'll have to help me too, because Mother will demand I be seen and not heard."

"About that," said Levi with difficulty. "About your mother?"

A long silence fell. Eventually, Deborah said, "Leah has a big mouth."

"And thank God *that* doesn't run in the family," said Levi.

"I can't tell you. Mother and I made an agreement."

"Deborah."

"It's the only reason she lets me work on *this*," she said. "And I had to build a whole extra *room* for it. You see that door?"

"Deborah, I'm your father. I asked you a question."

"And she's my mother."

Levi sighed. "When I come back, I'm not good with people. I can't read expressions well. I don't know what's going on. I need you, Deborah."

Even as he said the words, Levi realized he was almost encouraging his daughter to lie to him. But he didn't think she would.

"Mordecai," she said.

Levi felt a sudden ringing in his ears, a whoosh of blood in his head. He staggered and Deborah was there, adroitly twisting her shoulder under his hand so he could lean on her. "Oh," he said, blinking rapidly. Of all the people Rebekah could have got herself immorally involved with in his absence: *Mordecai?*

"So, *you* be careful," said Deborah. "And, come on. We really shouldn't leave her alone with those gorgeous men any longer."

Levi put his other hand on the twin-wheeled conveyance. "What do you call it?"

"What, this wooden thing?" Deborah said, and stood primly upright, mimicking the angels. "'It Has No Name.'"

"No, really."

"I, uh, call it my Wooden Ass," she said. "But as you might imagine, that's not something I've shared with anyone else."

Levi laughed again. Damn the Deeps, damn its infernal—sacred—machines. His family was here; this was the real world. "I'll smooth things over with your mother. I'll make sure you can keep this, find you time to work on it. I could even help you develop it … but only if you want me to."

Deborah smiled. "All right."

She fastened the door closed, and they walked back around the house. Levi said, "Remember, I just scolded you. Try to look less happy."

Deborah grinned again, then her face slid back into the sullen expression of resentment she'd worn when he first arrived. "Yeah. Lousy father. Overbearing jerk."

"Arrogant slut," said Levi.

They hugged briefly, out of sight of the house windows, and went back inside.

✧

"God is not so apparent in all His Houses…" "As He is to you, in this one."

"I see," said Levi, cutting mutton and putting a piece in his mouth. The angels seemed perturbed at having to touch the meat with their fingers. He wondered what—and how—they usually ate. He was mildly surprised they ate at all.

He looked around the table. His family chewed industriously, not looking up. They'd picked a fine time to lose their tongues. "And so, you are from another House?" he prompted.

One nodded. "We are visitors," said the other.

"And so this is not the first time you've been out of Heaven?"

They sat very still, columns of white and blue. Unlike his daughters there was no fidgeting, no scratching, no drumming of fingers or heels. Perhaps each was waiting for the other. Or perhaps they had no answer.

Levi persisted. "You didn't expect it to be like this, did you? Here in Shadom?"

"It's very nice here," said one, politely. "But yes, it's very different." "Things change." "Variations."

"Like what?" he said.

One cleared his throat. "You are fishing."

"Fishing?" Deborah joined the conversation at last. "What is *fishing*?"

Shadom's water came from wells. Deborah had never been under the sea, never even seen a river. Levi had so much of Creation to show her. But he kept his face neutral, and waited for the angels to answer.

"Fishing is seeking information through careful questions."

"And we shouldn't do that?"

Rebekah flicked at Deborah with a cloth. "Speak only when you're addressed, daughter!"

"Please," said Levi to his wife, and then to the angels, "If you are uncomfortable with questions, please tell us. We wish only to serve God as best we can. More corn?"

"And to understand," said Deborah sweetly, "just what it is you want with my father. Assuming it's my father you're interested in." Provocatively, she held eye contact with the leftmost angel.

Rebekah picked up her cup of water and dashed it into her daughter's face. "For shame! Leave our table! Did I raise you to be a jezebel?"

Levi raised his hand. "Hush…."

He fully expected Rebekah to turn on him next and blast him with her frustrations. "And *you*!" she might have shouted, "After the better part of a *year* you just walk in unannounced and expect to be treated as the head of this household?"

Rebekah did turn to him. But she spoke quietly. "See? She's doing it to us again. And every single time, you fall for it."

And Levi understood. Almost since the day of her birth, Deborah had been devious. Precociously smart, she had mastered the skill of playing her parents off against each other. And even today, he now realized with a sinking feeling, how adeptly she'd distracted Levi from his questions about her behavior by taking him to see her wooden ass.

What more natural strategy for Deborah than to distract Levi from her own sin by accusing her mother of a bigger one? Was Levi proving himself a bigger fool with every passing minute?

He looked at Deborah. He had trusted her, given her permission to speak at table, and she was using it to flirt with the angels. Or was she just so mired in her own depravity that she couldn't control herself, faced with creatures of such beauty?

Deborah pushed her chair back. As she wiped the water from her face, the shawl fell from her bare shoulders. She seemed very calm. Why wasn't she shouting back at her mother, like usual?

Because she didn't need to. She gestured minutely across the table.

The angel was blushing.

"Deborah, leave the room," said Levi curtly.

"What?" Deborah raised her arms in outrage, and with a smooth motion Levi rose to his feet, seized his daughter's wrist and dragged her away into the kitchen area.

Frustrated, she punched him on the shoulder. He put his lips to her ear. "It's all right. I saw."

Deborah's face contorted with feigned anger, and she hissed back, "Something isn't right. Why would a true angel of the Lord be tempted by *me*? If they were pure, would they look at me twice? And if they have no virtue, then what are they?"

"We can hear you, you know," one of the angels said mildly.

"And we admire your ingenuity," said the other.

"If not your honesty."

"Oh well." Deborah turned and smiled right at Rebekah with an almost malevolent expression, and with a sick feeling Levi realized his home life had gone to Hell in a grass basket.

Instantly, Rebekah was on her feet. "You two! You two! What is it always between you two?" She picked up the dish of corn and aimed it, and with a scream little Leah slid off her chair and hid under the table against the coming storm.

And that was the precise moment when the first rock hit the front of Levi's house.

☼

More Crass-men now, close to twenty of them, lined up across the street like a challenge. Levi saw pots in their hands, amphorae of mash beer. Even from here he could smell it on them. Nearby stood a squad of pouting jezebels, grouped together for safety, creatures of small intelligence and perverse appetites. And children, youths, more arriving every moment.

The sun was setting behind the mountains. Despite the evening warmth the adjacent houses were shut up tight without even a candle burning in their windows, as his neighbors carefully minded their own business.

Naturally, there was never a Justiceman around when he needed one.

"What do you want?" said Levi to the mob.

"Your guests." A tall bulky Crass-man stepped forward with a leer, and with a small shock Levi recognized Mordecai, his wife's alleged lover.

He tried to push it from his mind. It was not relevant to their current danger.

"My guests are my guests," Levi said mildly. "You have no business with them, I believe."

"Keep 'em all to yourselves, would you?"

"Bring 'em out," called a jezebel. "We just want to see 'em. Our competition. With *them* here, nobody's looking at us twice."

Levi had no doubt which way this was going. "You would offer violence to servants of the Lord?"

"Who said violence? We just want to look."

"Pretty boys, pretty boys," said a Crass youth not much older than a boy himself. "Bring 'em out, we say." He took a swig from the amphora he carried, and passed it to the next man on the line.

"Blue skin," said a woman. "Not natural, is it?"

Levi glanced back at the doorway of his house. Fortunately, the angels had the wisdom not to show themselves. "They're under my hospitality. My protection."

Mordecai stepped forward. Levi stood his ground, gripping his staff till his knuckles whitened. "Levi, oh master Levi," said the Crass-man. "We all know you're good as gold. But not so smart." He rapped his knuckles against his own forehead. "No common sense, not even with your own family."

"My family are my business."

"They're your *first* business," said Mordecai. "Those pale men are nothing to you. You think they're angels? They're not angels. Angels are going to come *here*, to Shadom, to see *you*? No, they're not, and you know it as well as I."

"Angels or not, they're still under my roof."

"They don't have to be," said one of the other men. "Bring 'em out, and you go back inside. Enjoy your evening. And we'll enjoy ours."

"Hospitality is a sacred trust," said Levi. He braced himself, feet apart, his staff grounded in the dust by his side. "I would sooner yield up my daughters than allow a hair to be harmed on the head of a guest."

"Oh, great," came a caustic female voice from behind Levi. "Thanks a *lot*."

Deborah had arrived. Mordecai smiled nastily. "Evening, miss. How's your *mother*?" He leered.

"Oh," said Levi involuntarily.

"See?" Deborah muttered. "You thought I'd invent something like that?" Stepping forward, she addressed the Crass-man. "Sir. My mother sends her fondest regards, and we'll need a moment to discuss your generous offer. We won't make you wait long."

Levi stared at his daughter, baffled.

"Come on then, Dad," she said, turning on her heel and stalking back toward the house. "Family discussion."

❂

Levi was shaking as he closed the door behind them. "I can't *believe* how you talk to men," he said to Deborah. "It's not…."

He stopped, dazed by the hive of activity before him. The angels were already boarding up one window, Rebekah and Leah the other.

"Well, don't just stand there," said his wife. "Nail the door shut and pull the cupboard in front of it."

"Family discussion?" said Levi.

"None needed," said Deborah, seizing a plank. "For the first time in my entire life, we're all agreed."

"They shan't have them," said Rebekah. "Give angels up to the mercy of Crass-men? God would turn away. We'd be forever damned."

"You asked me for sanctuary," said Levi to the blue men. "Before you even asked for hospitality. 'Sanctuary', you said. Because you knew this would happen. You intended it. You put my family in danger."

For once the angels did not look convincingly innocent. "We are in danger also." "Do we not bleed, just as you do?"

"Then this must be important," he said roughly. "Why don't you tell us *why*?"

"We shall," said the Beautiful Ones. "Just as soon as we've boarded up your windows."

The pounding was almost deafening. "And you think they can't hear this outside, what you're doing?"

"It'll take the Crass-men a while to warm up," said little Leah. "First they'll shout and throw things some more. Then they'll drink more beer and wait for the sun to go down. We have time before they get *really* angry."

He stared at his little girl. "Oh, Leah."

Deborah nodded. "Tousle-head is right. A challenge will make their victory all the sweeter."

"Why do I go away?" said Levi, desperately. "Why do I allow myself to miss your growing up?"

"I don't know," said Deborah. "Why do you?"

"You're asking *us* this?" said Leah, who was all set to grow up just as difficult as her sister. "And *now*?"

"I'll not see them harm you," said Levi.

"Leah," said Rebekah. "More nails."

Levi walked close enough to murmur in his wife's ear. Even approaching her was an effort. "And while I was away, you lay with *him*?"

"For God's sake," said Rebekah. "For once in your life, stop talking and *do* something."

❂

"Your God is testing you," said the Beautiful Ones.

"Don't you mean *our* God?" Deborah said quickly.

Levi held up his hand. "Why are you really here?"

The blue-white men looked at each other with identical blank expressions, and sighed indistinguishable sighs. "God will destroy this city."

"Oh," said Levi. Rebekah sat down suddenly, just as Leah had done a couple of hours earlier, but on a stool.

"God will destroy Shadom." "And we need to get you out of here." "Before it happens."

Levi shook his head. "Nonsense."

"How many in this city truly believe in Him?"

"All of them," said Rebekah.

"Fifty?" said the angels. "Twenty of them?" "Ten?" "Five?" "Name five truly virtuous men, and maybe God could be persuaded to spare Shadom." "But you, Levi—" "You are God's agent in this reality." "You work the heights." "You work the Deeps." "You are God's Engineer."

The continuous back-and-forth was hypnotic. Levi felt like he should concentrate just a little harder. "Engineer?"

Rebekah snapped, "God is *here*! We see His work around us every day!"

"But you do not see *Him*." "Less easy to worship a God you cannot see."

"Worship?" said Levi. The word was unfamiliar, but it sounded profound.

The angels looked at each other. "Praise." "Adore."

"You *praise* God?" said Deborah.

They blinked. "Most believers do." "We do not need to, personally…" "The words we use may be unfamiliar." "From the outside, God's work looks different." "God's house contains many mansions." "Different strokes."

Levi rapped his fist on the table. "Enough. Back to 'Destroy this city'?"

"Yes." "Yes."

"We should live that long," said Rebekah, glancing at their boarded-up windows.

"God won't do that," said Levi. "Listen. When I leave Shadom, I do God's work. He speaks to me. Tells me what to do, watches me do it. I don't remember it well, but I do *remember* it. I have … an *advantage* when it comes to belief. The people who live in Shadom, who work the crops and the goats and trade with the desert caravans, it's not always so clear to them."

They shrugged. "Not relevant."

"Of *course* it's relevant," Levi said. "God couldn't harm them for doubting Him, when He doesn't *show* Himself to them!"

"Why do you still think these angels are really angels," said Deborah, "when they're not even describing the same God?"

"It is the same God!" said one of the angels forcefully.

The other one cleared its throat. "God has a lot invested in you, Levi."

"Invested?"

"You are special." "Good artisans are hard to find." "You must be begotten, not created." "For creativity itself cannot be created." "You understand?"

Deborah leaned forward. The angels looked worried. "Explain more clearly," she said. "If you're perfect, it shouldn't be hard to choose perfect words."

"And you have only minutes to convince us," Levi added.

As the darkness grew, it was as if the angels shone from within. Their faint silver-blue reflections glimmered from the glazed pots and cups. "Very well." "We will try." "It is not as easy as it may appear to create and guide a being with free will." "If obedience is mindless, it is worthless."

There was a long pause. "That's it? We're supposed to understand that?" said Levi.

"It's a fine balance," said one of the angels almost apologetically.

"But, if people disobey only out of ignorance…."

It was Deborah's turn to rap on the table for attention. "So you can keep us safe? The men outside, who want to, well, do wicked things to you. You can protect yourselves from them? And keep us safe as well?"

The angels looked fearfully at the window, and then at Levi.

"I'd say that's a 'No'," said Leah.

Rebekah slumped, her head in her hands.

Deborah walked up to them. "You're very beautiful. And you're absolutely frigging useless."

Levi felt a familiar prickle at the back of his neck. With a sudden clarity, he knew what was about to happen. But not why.

"Here's how this is going to work," he said. "We save you from the Crass-men. Then you save us from the destruction of Shadom."

One angel glanced upward conspiratorially, and nodded. The other looked relieved. "Get us to high ground."

"I thought this conversation couldn't get any stupider," said Rebekah. "But then, all of a sudden?"

They all jumped as a pot exploded into smithereens on the roof. The cat-calling outside their house was turning into a baying that Levi had never heard out of human throats.

"Don't believe them," Deborah said to Levi, in some desperation. "You make it so much easier for them when you put the words right into their mouths. Trust me, I know how that works." She still stared at the angels from close range, right on the edge of igniting into fury. If that happened it might take another ten minutes for Levi to regain control. And they might not have ten minutes.

Levi walked up to his daughter and put his hand on her shoulder. She stiffened, but did not twist away.

"Let them be. I have an idea to get us out of here, Deborah. But I can't do it without you."

✧

Out from the lean-to crashed the most ungainly vehicle ever glimpsed in Shadom. Deborah rode it, Levi's scandalous hussy of a daughter, her legs astride it, one hand steering while the other pumped the lever-handle that drove the back wheel harder and the wooden ass faster than it could otherwise go. Behind her on the seat her little sister clung to her back, screaming incoherent but gleeful words of encouragement as they sped over the bumpy streets of the city.

In the cart behind were the two blue-white men, their faces seeming even whiter with alarm in the dusk half-light. Swaying dangerously, they kicked backward against the ground to help scoot the vehicle along. Deborah was strong, but not quite strong enough to propel the four of them faster than a man could run, all by herself.

The mob cried out in shock. For all the ass's shakiness, it was still absolutely the first human-powered getaway vehicle they had ever seen. The sheer surprise factor allowed the fugitives to ride fifty feet beyond the unruly throng of Crass-men and jezebels.

Mordecai leaped forward with a roar, as if meaning to chase down the wooden-ass cart himself. He could probably have done it, too; of all the men there he was the strongest and fittest. But Levi walked out of his house with Rebekah two paces behind him. The patriarch and his wife strode up to Mordecai and confronted him, their faces as stern as their rapidly-receding youngest daughter's screeches were gleeful.

Only then did the other Crass-men recover, the younger men setting off pell-mell after Deborah and the blue angels.

"Should have fled with your whore of a daughter," said Mordecai. "You skinny joke of a man, nose in the air? Leaving your family to fend for how long, while you gallivant in the hills? Should've scarpered with your bum-chums, oh yes."

"No," said Levi. "Because I'll do whatever I must, to keep my family and my guests from harm. But I will never turn my back and run from a man like you."

"Gone too far, this, now, see?" said Mordecai. "We'll put you back in your house, and we'll seal it up with your own hammer and nails, tight as you like. And we'll burn it down with you inside. And then, off we'll go after those comely creatures of yours, who won't get so very far out in the desert, and we'll do to 'em what we were set to do all along. And they'll die on their knees, your daughters included. And that's how this ends."

"Which reminds me," said Levi. "Nobody calls my daughter a whore."

"Except me," muttered Rebekah.

Mordecai laughed, while Levi's neck prickled even more. "A whore, I say! And you know what, Levi?—she's the daughter of a whore! What d'you say to that?"

"Well, nothing," said Levi. "But I'll have to—"

And in mid-sentence he whirled his staff, catching Mordecai hard on the side of the head. Because clearly Levi had to fight, but when faced with an adversary of Mordecai's bulk even an ethical man had no call to fight fair.

Mordecai howled and staggered, and the remaining crowd—those not chasing after the comely behinds of the Beautiful Ones, or standing scattered with their hands on their knees panting after giving up the chase—howled too. In their case it was with glee, for they loved a good fight and so rarely got to see one.

Levi whacked Mordecai again, and Mordecai raised a fist like a ham and thumped Levi back, knocking him fifteen feet across the road to sprawl headlong into the dirt.

On the ground, his head spinning, Levi heard Mordecai's approaching footsteps and the sound of a blade being unsheathed. A modicum of self-defense was called for, but Levi was too dizzy to do any more than prop himself up on his forearms. The odds of him getting up before Mordecai arrived seemed remote.

An unearthly screech went straight through Levi's head. His first thought was that he had never heard Rebekah make such a sound. Then a profound black stench washed over him, followed by a gory wet *crunch*, and a man's scream cut off before it even got properly started.

Levi looked up to see the men and women of the mob scatter and tumble as Lilith dragged the corpse of Mordecai through their midst. Soaring sharply upward, the demon shrieked again and ripped, and a rain of blood and meat pattered down across an area the size of the city square. A disembodied arm bounced off the roof of Levi's house.

He stood, trying not to vomit. None of the leaderless mob seemed inclined to challenge him further. Rebekah had taken three steps toward the epicenter of the falling gore, her hands up to her temples.

"We have to go," he said. "Come *on*."

"I'm staying," Rebekah said dully. "Mordecai. Someone has to clean him up."

"Let his friends do it."

Rebekah closed her eyes. "Please, Levi. Don't make this any harder than it is already."

"But," said Levi, waving his arms, "the girls!"

"*Your* girls. I've looked after them long enough. It's your turn now."

She stood before him, a pillar, unbreachable. Levi saw no softness in her, no tears. Only bitterness and salt.

"You really lay with Mordecai?" he said.

"You're not here. You're never here!"

"I'm here now!"

"Not for me," she said. "I don't want you any more. Just go chase after your damned daughters, Levi. Don't come back."

"Gladly." Levi turned in the direction the wooden ass had fled, toward the city gate he had entered through just a few hours earlier.

A gate which, he now saw, was closed. With his daughters and the angels still on this side of it.

"Crap!" shouted Levi, and began to run.

Next moment, the claws of Lilith wrapped him and dragged him high into the darkening sky.

✿

"Open the gate," growled Lilith. "Or I'll have to knock it down. And that would be work."

The desert spun dizzily hundreds of feet below. Lilith's insane speed had carried them over and past the wall and she was looping back around. Clamped by the right thigh and the left shoulder, Levi could not twist to look up at her, only down at the hard shadowy ground. The wound in his leg cracked open, and his blood once again began to flow.

Despite everything he still clutched his staff, and now he remembered what it could do.

Maybe it was the altitude, or being outside the city walls, but the knowledge of God's Engineering that had dropped away from Levi on his return to Shadom came back in a rush.

As Lilith swooped, Levi's vertigo vanished. Just inside the wall he saw a small flash of blue and a handful of ants running toward it; Deborah's cart ('rickshaw', said a voice inside his head) had stopped at the gate and the young bucks at the vanguard of the mob were approaching them at speed.

"Put me down on the left side," he said. The gate grew in front of his eyes, and then Lilith dropped him onto the wall and Levi ran full tilt for the guard-house, his cloak streaming out behind him.

Three guards awaited, one still clutching a wine-skin even as he drew his blade with his other hand. Still running, Levi pressed a whorl on his staff and a whoosh of flame shot out over the guards' heads. Immediately all resistance crumbled. The guards dropped the knives, and Levi snarled "Open the gate!" which, obligingly, they turned and did.

Tanned faces had turned upward. Nobody had missed the gout of fire that Levi had magicked out of nowhere. The gate creaked open and, thirty feet below, Deborah calmly sat back down on her wooden ass and drove the angels out of the city of Shadom.

Levi slid down the ladder to the ground and faced the dozen Crass-men who awaited him. They fanned out around him.

He looked at his staff. He well recalled the fire he had made with it just moments before; the afterimages still fluttered in his eyes. But Levi was back at ground level now, and only smart enough to realize that there was something he had already forgotten. God's knowledge had left him just as abruptly as it had arrived.

The mob, of course, didn't know that.

"Come on, then," he said. "Who wants to burn first?" He brandished the staff in what he hoped was a competent street-fighting stance.

Above them in the night, Lilith roared by. An odor of dankness washed them. The mob hesitated, and Levi said scornfully, "Really, lads, just go home," and walked away through the gate.

They let him go. The gate crunched closed behind him with impressive finality.

✧

If he had run, Levi could have caught up with his daughters and angels in no time. Yet he chose to be alone, to contemplate the enormity of what had happened. Once reunited, it would take Leah only moments to ask, *What now, Daddy?* And Levi wanted to have an answer for her by then.

Besides, if Levi ran the way he usually did outside the city, he could crash into them at speeds they might not survive, which would at least have been the birth of Irony in this particular mansion of God's Creation.

So Levi trudged on, calming himself, trying to rationalize a capricious world.

A philosophical calm that lasted all of five minutes before his neck prickled furiously and Lilith snatched him away from the ground once more.

✧

"Are you going to kill me?"

"You're still alive," said Lilith. "Think about it."

She stood before him on the mountainside, gaunt, ugly, marbled with muscle, chokingly female. Lilith was screech-owl, baby-slayer, succubus and seed-stealer, plunderer and destroyer, and the blazing bonfire beside her only amplified her stench.

"Are you Temptation, then?" he said doubtfully.

She cackled, and shimmied in an abhorrent parody of flirtation. "Why? Are you tempted?"

Levi stepped back.

"I am Retribution," she said. "I am Destruction. You don't find me beautiful?"

"I...." Levi took a deep breath, wondering how such a misshapen creature could be so charismatic. "I find you impressive."

"Not a lie, and yet not the whole truth," Lilith said cheerfully. "Well spoken, Levi."

"My daughters?"

"Will follow the light and join us presently. And then we'll go higher. But for now, how about a fireside chat?"

Levi peered down off the mountain into the shadows.

"Nothing will harm them," she said. "My word on it."

"What *are* you?"

"Ah, the eternal question." Lilith preened, a giant predatory bird. "God fashioned me with His own hands. I was His first woman. Not long afterward, He created camels. Since then I've been helping to clean up His other mistakes."

"Mistakes?" Levi followed a God who could suffer a Lilith to live? "May I sit down?"

Lilith gestured generously. "This world, too, is one of God's first tries. Even with your valiant behind-the-scenes efforts to shore up its foundations, He couldn't stabilize it. His more recent attempts at world-creation have been more successful."

"And the angels?"

Lilith laughed mockingly. "*I* am God's avenging angel, and always have been. They are only angels by the lights of *their* world. Which is to say they're fondly imagined, rarely seen, always over-interpreted, and largely ineffectual."

"They spoke of destroying Shadom. But since they could barely drive in a nail, even with both of them holding the hammer...."

"Oh, they can't destroy anything," Lilith agreed. "But I can."

She gestured at the sky. And, not two hours after nightfall, the sun rose again.

Levi toppled with a cry, shielding his eyes. The baleful crimson orb that lurched back above the western horizon was not the sun he knew, nor could it reappear in such a position unless Lilith had torqued the entire world. Yet there it was, the color of brimstone.

"And that isn't even the best part," said Lilith. "Observe if you please: the dawn of the titans."

Giants were shambling in from the west, huge beings, hundreds of feet tall. Shaped like men, yet not men, unless men were fashioned from dirt with sigils of doom carved into their massive flat foreheads.

"Golems," Levi breathed. Striding toward Shadom, carrying immense pails that bubbled and steamed. The ground beneath the colossi sizzled when they slopped. "No. I beg you—"

"Beg till you bleed, Levi. They answer to a Master mightier than you or I."

Levi estimated their distance and speed. For all their size it would take the titans over an hour to arrive at Shadom. But what could he do in an hour?

"Tell me," said Levi urgently. "The angels spoke of worship. I need to know how to do that."

"That's a later idea. It won't work here."

"But—"

"Levi." Lilith leaned forward, her beak of a nose right up in his face. He would have recoiled from such ugliness, and from the musky stink that came with it, if he had not been captivated by the deep compassion in the demon's eyes. So Levi stayed where he was, his own eyes wide and unblinking as he inhaled her primal femaleness, and from close range he barely understood her words. "Levi, in your heart you must already know. God has already left the building."

And so all that Levi could do was watch and wait.

For all his horror, there was a certain fascination to the golems' advance on Shadom. The men arraying to defend the city walls looked puny, the line of people fleeing eastward slow and futile.

Lilith gave no order, and Levi saw no signal given, but down on the plains the foremost of the titans stepped forward, reached into his pail, and flung a heavy pawful of brimstone.

The wall fizzed. Houses exploded. The Misbegotten-of-God fell on Shadom in mighty waves.

It took free will to create, but none to destroy. Perhaps mercifully, darkness and clouds soon obscured the city's fiery end.

☼

The bonfire was merely embers and glow by the time the others tramped into camp: Deborah and Leah holding hands, and several minutes behind them, two white-blue beings who finally had the grace to look dusty. Levi waited for their sarcastic comments about him taking it easy while they slogged uphill all night, or perhaps about his consorting with demons, but his daughters merely slumped into his arms to be hugged.

None of them looked back toward the scorched plain where Shadom had once lain. Nobody mentioned Rebekah's name.

Lilith cleared her throat. "Well. Now we're all together, shall we go on?"

☼

The cave was square, and eerily illuminated with a silver-blue radiance.

This was not how Levi had imagined it. Not the way his faded, holey memories had led him to believe.

For one thing, it was all much smaller than he remembered. The machines of the Lord were huge, but not larger than the mountains they had helped him move. The pit beyond was deep, but it was not an abyss that could swallow worlds.

The vehicle that rose up by his side was indeed immense—on seeing it his daughters had taken it for just another wall, until Deborah had realized that the disks within its giant treads were wheels—but it was silent and inert. And God's voice was not in Levi's mind to guide him. Although Levi had the sense of having been here before, he viewed it through a lens dark and cold, devoid of the Lord's warming breath. The power of these machines did not stir him; the vital knowledge did not whirl across his brain. Here stood Levi, God's Engineer, as useless as the machinery that surrounded him.

Levi could not even recall how to get into the high room from which the silver beast was controlled. He knew that once the raucous din of its engines filled his ears, it would be a craft capable of performing wonders. Perhaps even of repelling the titans that had destroyed Shadom? For a moment Levi's gaze lingered over its sleek lines, and the giant arm that rose from the body of the machine into the sky. If Levi had only gotten here sooner, if he could remember how to drive it, if he had maneuvered it down to the plains….

Such speculation was useless. The scouring of Shadom had been the Lord's will. Levi could not have stopped it, and so the deaths of his neighbors and friends, and even his wife, should not stain his conscience. Should they?

Other machines stood haphazardly around the enormous room, yet they seemed utilitarian and unwieldy, even … uninteresting.

But not to his daughters. Leah's and Deborah's eyes sparkled, flooding with joy; they gaped right and left, across and upward, struck mute with wonder. To Levi's girls, God's Garage was a paradise beyond imagining. Yet Levi could see Deborah assessing and analyzing, already making her best guesses about how everything worked.

Out in the middle of the glossy floor she turned and flashed him a reproachful look. Levi understood;

he had kept her away from this all her life. But he was giving it to her now.

✡

"God is an angry God." "A jealous God." "Implacable in His judgments." "Impatient with His mistakes."

Above them, the roof slid away. The clouds were also rolling back, to reveal a light-blue morning sky. Then, as Levi watched, the sky itself split, a jagged wound appearing over him like the tear in his own thigh. Beyond it he saw only a dim shifting haze.

"God's first worlds perished in flood, now this one will perish in fire." "Few are the things in this House that God would keep." "God strives to save the virtuous."

"Not the virtuous," said Deborah. "The *useful*."

Levi almost looked around for Rebekah to scold her daughter, and felt an unexpected pang that she had perished, burned away without a second thought. He turned on the angels. "My wife. If the Lord made her lustful and did not give her the strength to resist, how could He punish her for that?"

The blue men looked uncomfortable.

"And how could a merciful God destroy a whole city?" He gestured at Lilith. At the still-clouded plains below.

"His mercy is not infinite." "What if mercy is not His main motivation?" They paused. "Much, we admit, is unclear." "Perhaps you should ask Him yourself."

"What *other* motivation could He have?" Levi demanded.

For the first and only time, the angels spoke together. "Progress. Growth. Development."

Lilith said, "Your world was one of God's early attempts, Levi. Be reasonable."

"You're all monsters," said Levi.

"We are not *virtuous*," Deborah persisted. "You want us because we have minds of our own. Creative minds. We're thinkers, makers. We can have conversations like this."

"Yes," said one of the angels.

"And we can be useful to you ... somewhere else."

"Yes," said the other.

"And you're not really from Heaven, are you?"

The angels became very still.

"Yeah, we've known all along," said Deborah. "What, then? What type of creatures are in league with Lilith?"

They shuddered.

"You're very quiet all of a sudden. You're making this up as you go, aren't you? Angels, my—"

She looked at Levi. "Ass," he said.

There was a long pause. "We are *like* angels." "We are engineers." "Not so different from angels." "And not so different from you, either."

They paused again. "Sometimes we improvise." "But we *did* come here to rescue you." "The Lord has more work for you."

"And if we don't want to be useful?"

Lilith yawned. "Then stay and boil, or wander off into the desert with the caravans. Good grief. But recall: just because you go with them, doesn't mean you don't have to do anything *else* they say. Remember *choice*?"

✡

They climbed the tall arm of the mighty machine, hand over hand. Struts jutted from the crane's trunk and arm, forming a ladder.

Leah climbed first. Deborah followed just a step below, guiding her sister's feet onto the struts and guarding her in case she slipped. Levi came after, trying not to look down, astonished at his daughters' pluck. The angels were already high above them, climbing as if Lilith herself were biting their heels.

"You're not coming with us?" Leah had said to the demon.

Lilith had shrugged. "I already exist there. And my work here isn't yet complete."

"Destroyer," said Levi.

"Someone has to do it."

Deborah grimaced. "But what if we need you, there?" Levi looked at her, surprised.

"Then you'll find me." The demon reached forward and chucked Deborah's chin, patted Leah. Levi instinctively raised his staff to protect them, but Lilith just grinned toothily, her underbite jutting up like a mountain range as she said to his daughters: "Never doubt it: *you* are the Beautiful Ones."

To Levi she had said, "All the work you did in this sandbox was not wasted. Much has been learned. Future versions will be better."

"Tell me where we're going."

"It would be hard to describe." The demon stretched upward, and a now-familiar gust of putrefaction swept them. "Enjoy your flight. Kiss kiss, now."

And with that as farewell, Lilith had taken to the air and soared away, a malign black bird.

The angels had started climbing the crane, leaving Levi and his girls alone on the floor of God's Garage.

"Well?" said Levi to Deborah.

She looked contemptuously up at the retreating blue forms. "Not even as far as I could throw them. But Lilith…."

"I know," said Levi. Despite her fearsome exterior and her stench, or perhaps because of them, Lilith had the ring of truth about her.

Now, from on high, Levi could see the flaws in this version of Creation; the fudges and cracks, the paint-overs. He remembered working on some of them himself.

God could do better. Perhaps He already had. It was an odd thought.

Above them, without even looking to see if Levi and the girls were following, the angels stepped off the crane into the gap in reality and vanished in the haze.

Levi continued to climb.

He caught up to Deborah at the tower's tip. She was looking back at the ground beneath. "Wow. High."

At the edge of the rift, part of the blue sky was hanging down. Resisting the urge to touch it, Levi looked through and past it.

A cool breeze played with his hair, scented with herbs and another aroma which was pungent but not unpleasant. For a moment Levi beheld a swath of purple and a glimmer of gold that he thought must be the face of God. Then he saw lights beneath him through the rift, and gasped as perspective snapped in. There, as here, they were a *long* way up.

Levi could sense God now, or thought he could; just a mental nudge at his elbow, but whether from his own world or the new dark land before him, he could not tell.

The haze was clearing. Through the tear in the sky Levi saw a mountain range silhouetted against stars, and a sinuous silver pulse that might be a river or a lake. Cold fires glowed, scattered across the plains like jewels on velvet, each fire perhaps marking a dwelling, a home to someone.

Or, he thought dazedly, each fire might be a city.

They beheld another creation. Another mansion in the house of God. Sweat dripped down Levi's face.

It was time to leave the old world behind. Levi gathered his daughters in. "Ready?"

"No," said Leah, as Deborah said, "Yes."

"Just kidding," said Leah.

"Brat," said Deborah.

"Slut," said her sister.

"Girls. Some dignity, please."

Deborah hugged Leah. "Don't worry, tousle-head. Just enjoy the ride."

Levi put his arms around them. They fitted against him, snuggled against his side. They were growing up so fast.

Emptiness opened up around them. The future beckoned. He felt sticky and new. Smiling, his eyes wide open, Levi leaped.

He couldn't wait to see how it all turned out.

Coptright © 2011 by Alan Smale. First appeared in Realms of Fantasy, August 2011.

Alicia Cay is a writer of speculative and mystery stories. Her short fiction has appeared in Galaxy's Edge *magazine, and in several anthologies including* Unmasked *from WordFire Press and* The Wild Hunt *from Air and Nothingness Press. She suffers from wanderlust, collects quotes, and lives beneath the shadows of the Rocky Mountains with a corgi, a kitty, and a lot of fur. Find her at aliciacay.com.*

THE LAMENT CONFIGURATION

by Alicia Cay

Joseph Ledélice and Guillaume De'sper, creators of the famous *Oiseaux de Délice*, the most desired toy birds in all France, were lost in their despair.

"Joseph!" Guillaume cried. "Where is it?"

Joseph hurried from the first-floor kitchen into the front room, a steaming mug of freshly pressed coffee in his hands. The main room of their chateau, adorned in Rococo finishes and soft blue florals, served as both workshop and library. Guillaume stood over his work desk, tearing through wood shavings and design drawings.

"Guillaume, you look a fright. What's happened?"

"I can't find it!"

"Find what?" Joseph asked.

"The bird I keep in the bottom drawer, it's not there."

Joseph dropped into the armchair in front of his matching work desk with its curved cabriole legs, spilling hot coffee onto his hand. "Oh."

Guillaume stopped his rummaging and glared at Joseph. Guillaume's face was flushed, and his hair had come loose from the velvet ribbon that gathered his long mouse-brown curls at his neck. He was as close to tears as Joseph had ever seen him.

"Why do you say, *oh*?"

With trembling hands Joseph set down his mug. "Two nights ago, I worked on one of the old birds."

The high color in Guillaume's drained to pale. "What does this mean? *Dis-moi*." His fingers twitched, curling and uncurling in loose fists.

"Madam Sorciére, from the village, the one with the sickly niece—"

"I know who she is!" Guillaume snapped.

Joseph flinched. He hated fighting with Guillaume. "As we … or *I* … have been unable to make one of the birds since …." He let the thought trail off, unable to bring himself to say his beloved daughter's name. "I took one of the cast-offs, the *oiseau* in your desk with the broken wing, and I finished it with paint, to give to her. For her niece."

Tight ribbons of muscle flexed along Guillaume's jaw.

"It already contained a song," Joseph said. "From when I was still able to make …." He stared into the black surface of his coffee.

Before their daughter's long illness and death, he and Guillaume had been the most sought-after toy makers in all of France. Guillaume carved the delicate bird's bodies from rosewood, fashioned their wings from real feathers, then Joseph painted them in delightful designs of pattern and bright colors. The finishing touch was the bird's songs, breathed into them by Joseph: *la vie expirée*. He rose in the morning after each month's full moon, set the new birds upon his piano, their onyx eyes glittering in the first rays of early morning sunshine; almost alive, but not quite. He composed a tune for each of them, then lifted each tiny oiseau to his lips and exhaled their song into them. Their gold-dipped wings would flutter to life, and each bird would lift off from Joseph's outstretched hand to flap about his head or perch nearby on a bookshelf, greeting the morning with their *nouveau* song.

"Joseph, how could you?" Guillaume said.

Joseph swallowed hard and forced his eyes up to meet his partner's.

Every muscle in Guillaume's body was stretched as taut as piano wire. He looked poised to lunge across the room and throttle Joseph. Guillaume did not, but the desire to do so was clear in his eyes. "You must get it back," he demanded.

More often lately, Joseph had run into Madam Sorciére on his afternoon strolls to the village, and each time she asked him for a gift of an Oiseaux de Délice to bring a smile to her ailing niece's face Guillaume would not consent, however, fast opposed to the idea of making toys for charity when there were paying customers to see to. Joseph's heart was not so business minded as all that, so he'd assembled an oiseau for her in secret.

"How can I take back a gift from a dying child?" Joseph asked. "Anyway, the bird was bent and broken. We could not have sold it as it was."

"Not bent and broken," Guillaume seethed through gritted teeth. "Well loved! Did you even *listen* to the song in it before you gave it away?"

Joseph stared at the tips of his shoes, his cheeks warming. He had not. It hurt too much. His *esprit de la musique* had wilted as their daughter's health failed, and when she passed, so also had his ability to breathe life into the glittering-winged oiseau. Joseph shook his head. "No," he murmured.

Guillaume wavered on his feet, then sat heavily in his desk chair and buried his face in his hands. "It was *hers*," he said through his fingers. "It held the song you created for our sweet girl on the day she arrived in our home. I kept it back from her casket."

Venom tipped honeybees took to stinging Joseph's heart. At Amélie's graveside, Guillaume had buried all the birds they'd made for her over the fourteen years she'd blessed their home. Soon he'd stopped saying her name. Then, he'd stopped speaking of her at all.

Joseph rose, went to Guillaume, and placed a gentle hand on his shoulder. "You didn't tell me you'd saved one of her oiseau."

Guillaume pulled his face from his hands—the heat and rage had abandoned his gaze. "It was the only thing I kept."

Guilt and shame dueled within Joseph's spirit. After Amélie's passing, Joseph's love for his partner and the life they'd built had kept him going, even as Guillaume's heart hardened into bedrock. "I can fix this, Guillaume. I will pen a letter to Madam Sorciére." He returned to his desk and pulled out a sheet of parchment. "I shall explain the situation and see to it that the bird is returned in whole."

Worse than any conflict that had plagued their home for the last three years, Guillaume stood and left the room without another word.

Joseph watched him go, swallowing back the daggers of grief that threatened to slice his tender heart apart. How could he have done this? He'd given away their dear daughter's song.

✿

The next day's sun dawned, painting the sky in morning pastels of yellow and pink. Joseph took his morning coffee among the white peonies in the front garden, their rosy-citrus smell brushing his cheeks, when a young blond man—leather satchel hung on a shoulder—made his way up the cobblestone path toward him.

Joseph stood to greet the messenger, who pulled a small, wrapped package from his satchel, accepted the livre laid across his palm, and departed with a nod.

Relief flooded through Joseph as he hurried into the house. "Guillaume, she has returned it!" He grabbed a silver knife and cut through the wrapping.

Guillaume, who had spoken barely a word to Joseph all night, emerged from their bedroom still dressed in his sleeping gown. His eyes were wide, his mouth open as though about to let loose in excited expectation.

Joseph unfolded the attached letter. "Dear Sirs, please accept my deepest condolences, however—"

Guillaume snatched the letter from Joseph's hands and continued reading. "My niece has become so deeply attached to the bird you kindly gifted to her that she cannot be parted from it. It brings a smile to her face, and she has slept soundly for the first time in a fortnight, rising each morning to this tiny treasure's inspiring song. Fear not, *mes bienfaiteurs*, I am not without heart. Please accept the included sentiment as a token of my appreciation for your kindness. May it bring you delight in a time of despair." He looked up at Joseph.

Joseph unwrapped the package, found a small crate within, and pried off the lid. From a bedding of down he lifted a delicate wooden box. It was crafted of bocote wood, dark and fragrant, and embedded along its sides in pink ivory were patterns of connected shapes and scrolling flowers, all surrounded by inlaid strips of mother-of-pearl.

Joseph gasped. Madam Sorciére had made her own fortune creating only a single, stunning, treasure box per year. Her boxes were so desired, it was said even King Louis XVI waited to see if his name would be drawn in her annual lottery. Joseph understood now why this was; the box he held was the most beautiful thing he'd ever seen crafted by human hands. He turned it over. The treasure box was of good weight and appeared solid in every respect—no latch or hinge marred its surface. He pulled at the top, then tried to slide it off, but no side would budge. He held it up to Guillaume.

Guillaume let the letter drop from his hands. He grabbed fistfuls of his hair and pulled. "It's gone. She refuses to return it! We must go to her at once and demand it back."

"Maintain your reason, Guillaume." Joseph bent and picked up the letter. "We can hardly barge into this woman's home and take back the gift we gave her."

"That *you* gave her!" Guillaume's voice fell into full baritone. "Do not speak of *we*. I had no part in the departure of my daughter's only remaining memory."

Joseph took a deep breath and scanned the letter. "There's more written here. Listen. Her gift is a *puzzle box* designed to aid us in the mending of our grief, but … she offers a word of warning."

"*Warning!*" Guillaume stalked the length of the large room. He grabbed a Meissen figurine from a stuffed bookshelf lining the walls, then set it back down among the imported porcelains and well-worn books. When he turned back to Joseph, his eyes burned like a fire gone wild. "Tell me then, what is this warning she dares give us, *l'audace*?"

Joseph cleared his throat. "Two solutions are possible, always of a choice. Solved with love, the box will yield to you the *Delight* of your heart. Resolve the box with bitterness, and *Despair* shall be your only companion."

Guillaume strode over and pulled the puzzle box free from Joseph's hands. "What kind of gift contains a warning?" He ran his fingers over the box, digging his fingernails along its sides in search of a catch or seam. The box was entirely intact. "What madness has she delivered to us?" Guillaume was nearly hysterical. "She offers us resolution to our grief without solution?"

The small hairs on Joseph's neck rose in anxiety as he watched Guillaume's increasing lunacy. "*Mon mari chéri*, you must calm yourself now." He pulled the box back rom his partner's clutching grasp. Guillaume immediately took a deep breath and seemed to settle down.

Joseph sat at his desk and turned the box over several times. How curious. Holding it seemed to further some spark of insanity growing in Guillaume. But how to take Guillaume's attention from it in this moment? He set the box aside and turned in his chair. "Shall I make us some breakfast, then?"

Guillaume selected a Ming vase from the bookshelf and hurled it across the room. Joseph reeled in his chair and pulled his legs up as the vase exploded in yingqing-glazed pieces.

"If this gift of hers promises payment for my pain, then I want it now!"

"Take hold of yourself, Guillaume! I do not like this change that has come over you. Madam Sorciére may be elderly, and she presents kindly enough, but we do not know what *pouvoirs magiques* she possesses to create such stunning boxes. It would serve us well to be cautious in this matter." He eyed the box on his desk. "We should consider this gift before we go against her in haste or madness. This house needs no more despair in it."

"How could I know despair more than in this moment?" Guillaume's voice dripped with rancor. "You have given away our daughter's song in charity and left me with nothing." He spit these last words like arrows, and they found their mark in Joseph's heart.

Joseph's chin dropped to his chest, his shoulders hunching. Amélie had been abandoned at four months old, left on the doorstep of the village church. Joseph and Guillaume had adopted her and loved her deeply for the next fourteen years. More than wanting to make right the error of giving her song away, Joseph desired a spring sun to thaw the icy landscape that had taken hold in Guillaume's spirit.

He stood up straight and stared back at Guillaume, trying to muster an authority he did not feel. "You have had your fit and your say. Now you will listen to me. Go and dress for the day and let us think on this. We will eat and gather our wits about us in order that we solve this puzzle for the correct solution. Agreed?"

Guillaume turned on his heel and stormed into the bedroom. It was as good an agreement as Joseph would get from him.

Joseph picked up the puzzle box and shook it gently. No sound of loose things rattled inside, yet it felt as though something heavy shifted within. He chewed his bottom lip. Had they angered Madam Sorciére for requesting the return of their bird? Joseph knew he must hide this gift of hers away until his partner's composure returned. The puzzle box unsettled him, but Guillaume's volatile desire to solve it unsettled him more.

☼

Joseph woke from troubled sleep and reached across the bed. Guillaume was not there. He rose and slipped on his green-and-gold silk satin robe.

The chandeliers in the front room were lit, and a gauzy layer of smoke hung in the air. The smell of burnt rosewood lay heavy about the space. Joseph found Guillaume hunched over his work desk. His partner suffered from sleeplessness and often crafted late into the night, still working on the tiny birds that Joseph could no longer breathe to life.

As Joseph approached, he saw that it was no oiseau Guillaume worked on. The puzzle box sat on the broad plane of his work desk surrounded by carving tools and hand drills of every sort. "Guillaume, *mon Dieu*, what are you doing?"

Guillaume turned, sweat pouring from his brow. 'I must get this box open."

Joseph had stashed Madam Sorciére's gift out of sight behind a stack of books which now lay tossed and scattered across the floor. His hiding of the box had not helped the situation but had fed the feverish intensity that now blazed in Guillaume's eyes.

"This madness must cease." Joseph reached across the desk to grab the puzzle box. Guillaume jumped up, chair scraping harshly across the oak herringbone flooring, and pushed Joseph. Joseph stumbled back, his arms flailing for balance. He tripped and landed hard.

Guillaume towered over him, his blood-shot eyes glowing in the dim light.

"You are possessed," Joseph cried. He scrambled to his feet and lunged again for the box.

"*Laisse le!*" Guillaume grabbed the back of Joseph's robe and flung him away.

Joseph rushed at Guillaume, pushing past him. He grabbed the puzzle box and raised it above his head. Guillaume hurled himself against Joseph, catching him around the waist. A grunt of air fled from Joseph; the box fell from his hands and hit the floor. Guillaume threw himself on top of it, hiding it beneath his body.

Joseph pulled at Guillaume's shirt and hair. Guillaume threw back an elbow and caught Joseph in the gut. He crumpled to the floor.

Guillaume scooted away across the room on his knees.

Joseph sat up, panting. Now it was his turn. The madness of that small, gifted box had reached him at last. It clawed through his chest with flame in hand and kindled a pyre of rage. How could Guillaume not see all that he had done for him? How Joseph breathed for him alone? But no, just as Joseph's once-glowing magic had done, Guillaume had abandoned him. "*Dis-moi*, what has taken you from me?"

Guillaume howled. "There is nothing left, save the tepid promise of hope this box offers." Sobs ripped from his throat, the sound of his escaping sorrow, beastly and unhinged.

Joseph rose on his knees and grabbed several unfinished birds from the work desk. He hurled one at Guillaume's head. It hit a shelf, letting out an off-key note of dead song. "You will find nothing in that box"—he shot another bird through the air; Guillaume batted it away—"that *I* do not offer you!" Joseph threw the last bird. It hit Guillaume in the chest and rolled onto the floor. "You have everything—fortune, renown, all the love you could desire within reach! What more *est nécessaire*?"

"I need my daughter back!" Guillaume roared. "Wicked Fate has taken her from us, and the man you loved has gone with her."

Joseph sat back, the pyre of his anger reduced to embers, tears trickling from his eyes. "Amélie"—Joseph's voice caught on the dust gathered across her name—"is gone, mon amour."

Guillaume shook his head. "I can no longer see. I have lost my sight."

Joseph crawled across the floor to Guillaume. "Our dearest Amélie is gone. My magic is gone. But I am still here, Guillaume. I am still here. If your sight has fled, then I will be your eyes until it returns."

Guillaume's limbs loosened, and he lifted his head—his eyes wells of black sadness. He nodded slowly. "We have both lost so much, Joseph. I did not also mean to abandon you. I—I could not see the way forward." He pushed the box away from his body, then let it go. The box clattered to the floor.

Joseph and Guillaume held one another tightly as years of unspent tears and unmourned despair drained from them, staining silk.

Spent, they sat on the floor against the bookshelves, tears and sweat drying on their faces. Outside, the sun unfurled its light into the sky, casting a golden glow through the windowpanes and across their huddled forms.

"I do not know what overtook me," Guillaume said, his voice raw and cracked. "I miss her." He trembled in Joseph's arms.

Joseph wiped a fresh batch of tears on his sleeve. "If you'll hear it, I have been toying with an idea." Guillaume chuckled. Joseph smirked, then said, "I know you work on the oiseau still, at night when you think I do not see."

Guillaume dropped his eyes, his fingers playing with the hem of his gown. *"Oui."*

"It is said Madam Sorciére makes her boxes sing with tiny machines she places in hidden compartments in the bottom."

"Music, from machines?" Guillaume said.

Joseph nodded. "What if we created a small compartment in the hearts of our birds? They would not fly as such, but nestled beneath the chins of the children of France, their songs would bring comfort, the same as they did for our Amélie and Madam Sorciére's niece."

Guillaume squeezed Joseph's hand. "We could bring life into the world still, this way."

"Oui," Joseph said. "In honor of the adored daughter who brought us life."

Guillaume's face flushed in an ombre of pink hues. "This idea fills my heart with joy."

"Can you forgive me, Guillaume?" Joseph asked. "For giving away Amélie's song, the delight of our lives. For losing my *la vie expirée*, and—"

"No," Guillaume gently interrupted. "It is I who should beg for your forgiveness. In my blindness, *mon amour*, I could see naught but my own misery. Even in your grief, you gave to Madam Sorciére from your heart. That is where your magic comes from, and I have done nothing to help put it back." He squeezed Joseph's hand harder. "But I shall try."

Guillaume reached out and picked up the half-painted, purple-and-gold bird Joseph had thrown at his chest. He smirked. "Perhaps, no more throwing birds, eh?"

Joseph laughed, dried tear trails cracking on his cheeks. He placed a hand on Guillaume's, over the bird. *"Oui, mon chéri—"*

Wings fluttered against Joseph's palm, and he snatched his hand back in surprise.

The tiny oiseau, its onyx eyes rimmed in circles of gold paint, stretched its purple-feathered wings. Then it hopped onto Joseph's forefinger, twisting its head in curious angles.

Joseph raised the bird to his lips and blew softly. The oiseau closed its eyes as Joseph's breath ruffled the golden tips of its wings. Then a small sound, a chirp that was not a song—but a start—warbled from its throat. Joseph laughed, and the bird, startled, hop-flew from his finger and landed on the puzzle box laying at the men's slippered feet.

A small catch within the box clicked, and the lid began to unfold in separate parts, drawing back to reveal a compartment. Joseph and Guillaume gasped in unison.

Inside the puzzle box was a small metal contraption with little gears and tiny teeth. The last piece of the lid was attached to a ribbon, and as it fell away it pulled the ribbon, which in turn dislodged a lever on the contraption. Amélie's song, the one hidden inside the oiseau Joseph had given away, began to play.

Then the tiny toy bird—almost finished but not quite—opened its tangerine beak and began to sing, echoing Amélie's song in perfect warbling harmony, filling Joseph Ledélice and Guillaume De'sper's hearts with delight.

Copyright © 2023 by Alicia Cay.

MADRENGA

New York Times Bestselling Author
ALAN DEAN FOSTER

"Rip-roaring action sequences and the mystery of Madrenga's curious powers propel the story through a series of consistently surprising twists and turns."
—*Publishers Weekly*

May 2023

Jean Marie Ward writes fiction, nonfiction, and everything in between. Her credits include a multi-award nominated novel, numerous short stories, and two popular art books. Her most recent release is Siren Bridge, *the first in a new Gaslight Western series from Falstaff Books. The former editor of CrescentBlues.com, she is a frequent contributor to* Galaxy's Edge *magazine and ConTinual, the convention that never ends. Learn more at JeanMarieWard.com*

BRIDGING DIVIDES IN SCIENCE, MAGIC, AND LIFE: GALAXY'S EDGE INTERVIEWS NISI SHAWL

by Jean Marie Ward

While still a small child, Nisi Shawl decided they were a mermaid and spun a complicated story cycle to explain how they came to live in a landlocked town thirty miles from Lake Michigan. Although (as far as we know) no merfolk ever claimed them, the episode proved prophetic. Shawl has spent their adult life bridging seemingly unbridgeable divides. Like the child who found a way to rationalize a mermaid living on dry land, Shawl's fiction spans the divide between science and magic, creating plausible worlds where technology and enchantment coexist and support each other. Their first novel, Everfair, employs the tropes of Steampunk, the most Victorian of science fiction/fantasy subgenres, to craft an anticolonial narrative leading to an arguably better future. Shawl's nonfiction bridges chasms of a different sort. As a teacher, journalist, essayist, and author (with Cynthia Ward) of Writing the Other, they seek to democratize and diversify the literary landscape, helping writers craft characters with which all their readers can identify. Galaxy's Edge *spoke with Shawl about their writing current projects, including* Kinning *(the sequel to* Everfair*), as well as their continuing efforts to increase inclusiveness and further the presence of people of color in the science fiction, fantasy, and horror genres at all levels—and gathered a lot of writing tips along the way.*

Galaxy's Edge: When did you first realize you were a storyteller?

Nisi Shawl: I would not actually say I'm a storyteller. I wanted to be a writer, but I'm not sure that's the same thing. There are people who tell stories who are not writers, and people who are writers who are not necessarily storytellers. If I'm a storyteller, it happens by accident.

GE: Okay. How did you get from wanting to write to your first publications?

NS: By persistence, that's how I got there. I was writing while I was in college and submitting stories, and they were bad. They were horrible, and I just kept going. I eventually got to the point of being good enough to attend Clarion West. That was when I started actually making inroads in publication. So, by trying, by submitting, that's pretty much the only way you can do it. My first publication was by invitation. I was working for a zine which was called *Popular Reality*. It was sort of an underground newspaper. We received an invitation from MIT Press for an anthology called *Semiotext(e)*. I got something in that. That was my first publication. But otherwise, it was just try, try, try.

GE: If the old saw, "Write what you know", has any validity, you can write just about anything. You've been a student, a musician, an au pair, janitor, cook, artist, model, a seller of structural steel, and a bookseller. Which of your work experiences proved most useful in your current career as a writer and a teacher?

NS: Pretty much none of those. My take on that saying is, yes, you should write what you know. But you should also make sure that you know a whole bunch of stuff, and if you don't know it, find out about it. That's what I think of that old saw. The thing that helped me most in my career as a fiction writer is my career as a journalist, because that got me to whittle things down and get rid of what Vonda McIntyre called the weasel words—the qualifiers and the "not quite" words. It made me conscious of the point of writing, which is to reach someone else.

GE: What correlation did you find between writing songs and short stories?

NS: My progression as a writer was very deliberately from the short to the long. Poetry and songs were ways of getting into a feeling, an idea, and then expressing it. I don't think that there's anything else—other than I could do this quickly—that made a difference between writing poems and short stories and novels. Certainly, I had some great experiences as a punk rocker, and those probably helped. But that's the only connection I can see.

GE: Your biographies and interviews cite a wide range of literary influences. Nevertheless, two of the writers on the list surprised me: Raymond Chandler and Howard Waldrop. What drew you to those authors, and how have they influenced your work?

NS: Raymond Chandler is easy, because he's very strong on the vividness, the liveliness of the setting. His settings are all characters. Description is nothing about this was sitting here and that was sitting on top of it. It's all about vitality. That was what I was looking for in his work.

Also, from what I have read he, like me, was plot-challenged. He was writing in genres that are very plot-centered—crime, thrillers, mysteries, police procedurals, that kind of thing. Yet he was able to get through it without a really strong sense of plot. I read his stuff over and over to see how he did it.

As for Howard Waldrop, he was one of my instructors at Clarion West. So, of course, I imprinted on him strongly, because during that time I was wide open to different influences. But what I love about Howard's work is—how to put this? In writing, people talk about the subtext of a story. There's the action, the plot, and then there's the meaning, the layer beneath it. Howard's writing puts the subtext on top. That's the only way I can think of to describe it. He wrote one short story called "Why Did". It was based on "Little Moron" jokes, which are horribly ableist, but they were very popular in my childhood and also, I believe, in Howard's. His "Little Moron" story took all the troubling aspects of those jokes and surfaced them. I find that fascinating.

GE: Returning briefly to the subject of Chandler and mysteries, you've also written a mystery, "Little Horses" in *Detroit Noir*, and incorporated mystery elements in several of your short stories. Was Chandler an inspiration for those stories, or was it more a matter of using literary vividness as a way of making readers overlook any plot-challenged aspects of the narratives?

NS: Gosh, I would have to say the latter. I have never really aspired to write mysteries. I was invited to the *Detroit Noir* anthology by a friend, and I thought, "Well, I will have to learn how to write a mystery, won't I?" Because that was what they were publishing. So, I wrote it, and then I was like, "Wait, no, I can't have …. The kidnappers, if they're not wearing masks, that means they're going to kill the people they kidnapped." There were all sorts of things I discovered about the writing of mysteries. But I discovered them in the process of writing, not by reading someone else who had done it well.

GE: What prompted the leap from short stories to novels?

NS: That was planned. I don't know if this is going to make sense to anybody else, but the way I look at it, I have to be the same person writing the entire work. But time passes differently when you're younger than when you're older. So, in my youth, I was writing shorter things because I was only the same person for so long. I would change swiftly. As I matured, I became more stable as a person and a personality, and I was able to write poems, short stories, and novels.

GE: Your debut novel, *Everfair*, was a hell of a book. It was ambitious, dense, scholarly, complex, and worthy of all the accolades that it received. In particular, the societies and politics you describe are all too real. But then you went further. You did something I've never seen any other writer do: you commissioned a currency. How did that come about? What made you decide to strike a coin for your fictional country?

NS: It was actually inspired by something outside of my creation. I was friends with Vonda McIntyre, and one of the things that Vonda did as she realized she was dying was she gave a bunch of stuff away. To me, she gave a Krugerrand, which is the South African gold coin that was supposed to save apartheid. Someone had given it to her. She hadn't purchased it. And she thought that I would either get that this was a great joke, or I would be horribly offended. I was bowled over with laughter from just the idea of a Black person receiving this Krugerrand. But then I had to think, what could I do with it? That was where I got the idea of recasting it as a coin of Everfair. So, it was Vonda's fault. Let's blame Vonda.

GE: I've heard whispers that there may be another coin cast around the time of *Kinning*'s release. Do you want to speak to that?

NS: Oh, I have no plans to strike any more. I, of course, have devised a complete system of currency and what's on the obverse and which ones have higher value and which ones are bigger and all that. But I don't have the precious materials to make it.

GE: Where does your nonfiction fit into all of this? You are famous for *Writing the Other*, but you've also done reviews, essays, and you're a journalist. Do you see something like *Writing the Other* as a part of a larger conversation with your fiction or as an outgrowth of your desire to democratize and diversify fiction as a whole?

NS: I think it's the latter, but it's really hard for me to separate them, other than the thing I try to do with nonfiction is stir people up to action, whereas with fiction, I'm just trying to create some wild and amazing new world. So, I guess, with the nonfiction, it's a call to arms. I always try to end with some sort of positive action that people can take, how they can fix things, rather than just saying, "Oh, this is terrible." With fiction, I'm trying to say, "Oh, this is wonderful."

GE: Or can be wonderful, in the case of *Everfair*.

NS: Yes. Well, becomes wonderful.

GE: A complicated wonderful, for sure. This idea of sounding a call to action and increasing diversity and inclusiveness in fiction is not something new to your experience as a writer. Can you tell our readers a little bit about the work you've done with the Clarion West Writers Workshop and the Carl Brandon Society?

NS: My work with Clarion West began before the stuff with the Carl Brandon Society, because I'm a graduate of that program, and I became a board member, gosh, I'm going to say maybe in 1997 or '98. The thing about Clarion West is that it has been changing and evolving and becoming much more focused on inclusivity and framing diversity. Some of the stuff that has helped has been the selection of instructors and changes in how critiques are run. There are people who buy copies of *Writing the Other* and make sure that it's included in the students' packets every year. So, they give people the perspective of *Writing the Other* right away. It's very inclusive that way, but it wasn't always. If I've contributed anything to that, that's great.

For many, many years, I was the only person of color on the board. I stayed through the microaggressions, the unconscious slurs and all that, and just kept plugging away at my agenda, which was to make it better. As for the Carl Brandon Society, that is a non-profit organized specifically to support and further the presence of people of color in the science fiction, fantasy, and horror genres, and all the imaginative genres at every level, from audience to author, to illustrator, to publisher, editor, characters—all of that.

The society got started at Wiscon in 1999, with a bunch of us sitting around in a room conspiring. We were inspired by a Samuel Delany essay that had just come out, "Racism in Science Fiction." We put together reading lists. We decided to give awards, which were modeled on the Otherwise Award (then called the Tiptree Award): one for fantastic fiction that examines and explores the ideas of race and ethnicity, and one [for speculative fiction] by someone of a non-white background. We did that A few years later, we started the Octavia E. Butler Memorial Scholarships. We also provided a forum for people to talk. We did dinners and made the idea visible that there are people of color in science fiction, fantasy, and horror.

GE: One of the ways you've been making people of color visible in SFF is by editing anthologies of their work, such as *New Suns*. Are you planning to edit more anthologies in the near future?

NS: Well, yeah. Actually, *New Suns* has a sequel *New Suns 2*. I have released the table of contents It's coming out in March 2023. Once again, it fea tures original speculative fiction by people of color. Some of the authors are the same, and some are new. There are eighteen stories this time, instead of seventeen, because I dipped into my own fee. The introduction is by Walter Mosley, and the afterword is by Dr. Grace Dillon, who invented the term indigenous futurism.

GE: Cool! That's something to look forward to. But you're not just working on anthologies of other people's fiction. Another collection of your short stories will be published soon: *Our Fruiting Bodies*. Forgive me for saying so, but the title seems a bit too on the nose, given the events of 2022. What can you tell us about that collection?

NS: I would say that collection is at least two-thirds horror, or at least two-thirds of the stories could be seen as horror. They are reprints gathered from quite a wide array of publications, including one that was only audio. That story was not printed. There's nothing that's original to the collection, but there's a lot of stuff that people would have missed. I put together a table of contents, I sent it to the editor, and she said, "Well, okay, we won't have this collaboration. That's too messy, but everything else, yeah, you're right, and it should pretty much be in that order."

GE: That's quite a tribute to your own editorial expertise. Was collecting so much of your horror fiction into a single volume a deliberate response to the zeitgeist?

NS: I have a problematic relationship to the idea that what I've written is horror, but I'm going with it. As for the zeitgeist, the collection had nothing to do with the idea that there's forced birth, for instance. It had nothing to do with the fight for people to have control over their own reproductive rights, nothing like that. It was more along the lines of there is kind of an upswell in the horror genre of people of color—and specifically of Black people—coming to the fore. Have you noticed that?

GE: I don't read much horror. But I am reading more fiction by people of color because I'm seeing more of it out there, and what I'm seeing is really good. The situation reminds me of a something I was told when I joined the civil service. The gist was, if you wanted to get ahead as a woman, you had to be twice as good as a man. If you were Black, you had to be four times as good.

NS: That sounds right.

GE: And the writers of color coming to the fore right now are certainly rising to the challenge.

NS: Since you haven't read a lot of horror, I will tell you there's something going on with that. My awareness of it is filtered through the teachings of John Jennings, who is an illustrator, a comics artist, and a professor at the University of California. He talks about and writes about the ethno-gothic. What he says is that people are focused on Afrofuturism, but in order to get to the Afrofuture, people have to go through the ethno-gothic and have to examine and deal with the burdens of being enslaved, the burdens of living under a rule of terror. The ethno-gothic is where we examine those legacies, that luggage.

I'm conscious of it now. For instance, when I wrote a story called "Conversion Therapy," about one of my heroes rescuing one of the children she cared for from a summer camp that was trying to convert [the child] from lesbianism, I had the characters go past this body hanging from a tree. I deliberately tried to invoke lynching scenes, because I think recognizing that that pain exists is a step towards freeing us from it and moving on from it.

GE: How do you get from these concepts—whether you call them dark fantasy, horror, or dealing with the gothic—to middle-grade fiction? I understand you have a middle-grade novel called *Speculation* coming out soon. What's the connection?

NS: Again, I say I have a troubling relationship to the idea that what I write is horror. Just because there are dead people, does that mean it's horror? Come on, dead people are a part of life. They're all around us. I just write this stuff, and if people want to call it dark fantasy, I'll go along with that, sure.

[In *Speculation*] there is, well, it's not exactly a curse, it's sort of like a self hexing. In the book, the characters call it the burden of the Coles. The family name is Cole, and this is the burden they have put on themselves. The heroine has to help lift that burden, so to speak. I see it more as a spectrum than as a dividing line between this is horror and this is fantasy, and this is appropriate for children, and this is not. It's more of a spectrum, and my place on that spectrum depends on my audience's interpretation of it.

GE: How did you change your writing style to accommodate younger readers—or did you?

NS: I didn't really change it that much. I thought I would get more pushback for using long words or, as they called them in my neighborhood when I was little, big words. But I think that might be due to the fact my heroines are usually geeks. They're usually word nerds. They have an excuse for using big words, and I write very closely from their viewpoints.

Another short story in this vein that I wrote from the viewpoint of a 10-year-old is "Wallamelon." That was in my collection, *Filter House*. Another one would be "The Rainses," which was published in *Asimov's Science Fiction*. "The Rainses" had lots of ghosts in it. It was about a heroine who wanted to find the Underground Railroad route that her family had been part of. So, I'm used to writing about really smart kids, and maybe that helped.

GE: Well, you were a smart kid, so it's something you definitely know about.

NS: Yeah.

GE: What are you working on now?

Nisi Shawl: I am now revising *Kinning*, which is the sequel to *Everfair*. I turned in a draft November of last year. My agent and my editor got back to me in March and wanted certain things. They wanted more material. That's what I'm working on now. I'm doing other things too. I was putting together *New Suns 2* during that time, and writing articles, that kind of thing.

GE: Articles related to *Writing the Other* or on different topics?

NS: Both.

GE: What have you found to be the hardest part about writing a sequel, especially a sequel to a novel so celebrated?

NS: Thinking I'm going to mess it up. I mean, people do love *Everfair*. There were people who hated it, because eleven viewpoints. "That's too many. I have to think about this book. I don't want to think while I'm reading." Those are the kinds of things I heard from people who did not dig *Everfair*. But a lot of people did. Now I'm trying to do this other book, and will it be as captivating? Will it have a heart that beats along the same paths? Will people want to spend time with it? And that kind of doubt, that kind of … what do we call that when someone has the thought that they can't do what they used to do? Imposter Syndrome—that is the hard part.

GE: Is there anything you'd like to add? Soapboxes provided free of charge.

NS: One thing that you haven't asked about is advice for other writers. Here is my advice: Try stuff out, learn, and figure out if it works for you or not. Keep what works, get rid of what doesn't, and expect it all to change, because it will. So, if someone says, "Write every day," and you write every day and that's not working for you, don't write every day. But there might be a point in your life when you decide that you need to.

GE: Thank you.

NS: You're welcome.

GE: We'll end the interview here—unless you want to talk about whether or not you still want to be a mermaid.

NS: [Laughs.] I think I am a mermaid, okay? People call me a mermaid frequently, so yeah.

Copyright © 2023 by Jean Marie Ward.

Richard Chwedyk sold his first story in 1990, won a Nebula in 2002, and has been active in the field for the past thirty-two years.

RECOMMENDED BOOKS

by Richard Chwedyk

BENDING, BLENDING AND NEVERENDING

Station Eternity
by Mur Lafferty
Ace
October 2022
ISBN: 978-0-593-09811-0

There's been a lot of genre-bending and genre-blending going on in the SFF field recently, and it has gotten more than some of the old-timers in a tizzy. If a novel features cowboys and werewolves, do you shelve it with the westerns or with horror and fantasy? Or a romance set on a multigenerational starship? Or a whodunit set amid the faerie folk? Frankly, it's never bothered me. Usually, the science-fiction or fantasy element eclipses (I hesitate to say "trumps") the other genre element. Or at least it used to be that way. Doesn't matter. I appreciate the freedom recent authors have had to define for themselves the boundaries of their work. Anything that confuses the folks who live to put things into their "proper" boxes is all right with me.

What we've always cringed at in this business was described over seventy years ago as the "Bat Durston Syndrome": westerns dressed in space gear; private eyes with rayguns instead of .38s.

The publishers' promo department is trying to sell Mur Lafferty's latest novel, *Station Eternity*, that way. Don't be fooled. Yes, there is a mystery at the heart of this engrossing story, but Lafferty, if you'll excuse the expression, dodges the bullet.

Mallory Viridian, P.I., has moved to a self-aware, alien space station because she happens to be too good at her job of solving murders. Her problem is the collateral damage that comes with her success: people close to her keep getting killed. She sees it as a jinx which she might only beat by living in an alien environment. But more humans arrive at the station, and more murders occur. What's a private eye to do?

The great thing, of course, is that Lafferty never forgets to be a science fiction writer, and the solution to the mystery depends on the science fiction elements in this story. It's a fine tradition that traces back to the R. Daneel Olivaw/Elijah Bailey mysteries Isaac Asimov wrote in books like *The Caves of Steel*.

Station Eternity is a fine novel, well worth your time.

◆ ◆ ◆

The Terraformers
by Annalee Newitz
Tor
January 2023
ISBN: 978-1-250-22801-7

Although I've been looking forward to the release of this novel, I did so with a bit of trepidation. I'm more familiar with Annalee Newitz's journalism, and there are journalists who, when they turn novelist, forget which hat they're wearing. I'm glad to report that my fears were unfounded. This is a fine *novel*, filled with all the things readers enjoy in a good novel, especially science fiction readers.

I've been fascinated with the notion of terraforming since I first encountered it as a very young SF reader. Newitz seems to share that fascination at a number of levels: the reasons for doing it, the practical approaches to accomplishing such a task, and the questions more recently bounced around concerning the ethical nature of terraforming: if we make a planet more "earthlike," do we mess with the natural ecology of the planet we propose to transform? Or even the natural ecology of space itself? We might declare a proposed planet lifeless or barren, but is it? By what standards do we measure the suitability of a planet to be terraformed? There is a great quote from a made-up environmental rescue team handbook used as an epigram: "Rivers might turn out to be people. Don't make any assumptions."

And these questions are very much at the heart of the novel, explored mostly from the perspective of Newitz's protagonist, Destry. Her family has overseen the terraforming of the planet Sask-E for generations, and the responsibility has now fallen upon her. At a crucial moment, it is discovered that a volcano contains more than the usual exogeological "stuff": a whole city—a *populated* city, too.

The central storyline is fascinating enough, but there are many other elements to Newitz's world that excited my all-too-often-ignored sense of wonder, like the "nonhuman biologicals" that often take an active role in the story, like Zest the hybrid cow:

> When they flew slowly enough to hear over the wind, Zest always chose to vocalize. "Look at the stubborn river!" she exclaimed. They all looked down. Below them, a valley had turned this section of the Eel into a lake that bulged between the peaks, the water along its shoreline spreading into the rocky fissures like tentacles.

Yes, on Sask-E, cows (at least hybrids) really *can* fly. That's just a sample of what's going on here, and it moves along gracefully to a thoughtful and satisfying conclusion. Much has been made about finding a "new direction" for contemporary science fiction, beyond the grim dystopias and opaque rehashes of classic-but-outdated space operas with a few new hunks of hardware and a more diverse cast of characters.

If *Terraformers* is the new direction in which science fiction is going, we're in very good hands.

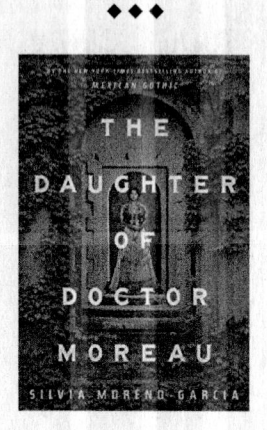

◆◆◆

The Daughter of Dr. Moreau
by Silvia Moreno-Garcia
Del Rey
July 2022
ISBN: 978-0-593-35533-6

I will not pretend that I "understand" this miraculous novel—not yet at least. But I may pay it what Vladimir Nabokov considered the highest compliment any reader can give any novel: I was—*am*—enchanted by it.

In no way is it a sequel or follow-up or updating or even a retelling, of that darkest of H. G. Wells's scientific fables, *The Island of Dr. Moreau*. The skeleton of the novel is there, moved to a different place and time. An eccentric scientist is conducting research on an estate in the secluded jungles, aided by an overseer named Montgomery Laughton Moreau's daughter, Carlota, also lives there. Moreau thinks the isolation is good for her nerves, though the evidence argues otherwise. Along with some servants and a couple of occasional visitors, the only other occupants of the estate are the "hybrids."

> "A hybrid. They are all developed in the womb of pigs. Once they reach a certain point of maturation, they are transplanted into this chamber. The solution is a mixture of a type of algae and a fungus which together excrete

certain chemicals that spur the growth," her father said. "The hybrid is also provided with a nutritive solution to ensure bones and muscles do not atrophy. There is more to it than that, of course, but you are looking at a creature that will have, in a few weeks, the ability to walk upright and manipulate tools."

"Then this is … you've mixed a pig with a man?"

"I've gestated an organism inside a pig, yes. And some of its gemules are from another animal, and some others are from humans. It is not a single thing."

These hybrids are not the product of the horrendous surgeries found in the Wells novel, and yet they are as strange and wondrous as anything to be found in that classic call against vivisection. Stranger, perhaps, since we can only speculate upon the hybrids' motivations, such as they are, or may be. They may be simple and apparent, or they may be complex and personal, and therefore hidden.

In both novels, Moreau sees himself as their leader, their creator, even their messiah. The difference is that in the original novel, the "House of Pain" is the dreaded place where the surgeries are performed (without anesthetics). In Garcia-Moreno's novel, the House of Pain is where the doctor performs his pseudo-religious services. The contrasts between these two "houses" leaves one to pause. The motivations of Moreau in both novels are as clouded and uncertain as those of his creations. The stated purpose, of course, is scientific research—to gain knowledge. But the behavior of Moreau in each case hints at something else. Isolated, lonely people, often create imaginary characters. Dr. Moreau, in both stories, transcends the imaginary. Both, in a sense, populate their own private worlds, and their creations reflect their creators.

In a significant way, the novel by Wells has become a myth, like the Frankenstein myth, and one that Moreno-Garcia finds particularly effective in exploring a number of topics, not least of which is the Caste War of Yucatán that took place in the second half of the Nineteenth Century. Human beings are arranged in a hierarchical pyramid for reasons that have little to do with practical needs and more to do with status and power (and the arrogance of power). In some respects, the situation also recalls the struggle of the "Underpeople" in some of the best-known tales of Cordwainer Smith.

The novel asserts its own reality in subtle and powerful ways. Even if you've never read, or even heard of, the H. G. Wells novel, Moreno-Garcia's work maintains a masterful tangibility. It is about loneliness and longing from a wide range of perspectives, reflected in the most simple of objects, places, and scraps of conversation.

Books like this are never read only once. This is the kind of book one returns to every few years or so.

I anticipate doing just that for many years to come.

◆ ◆ ◆

Deathless Gods
by P. C. Hodgell
Baen
October 2022
ISBN: 978-1-9821-9216-7

Let us now praise P. C. Hodgell. Because it's long overdue.

Hodgell has been laboring in the fields of her secondary world, following the peoples of the Kencyrath, especially her central protagonist, Jamethiel Knorth (better known to fans as Jame) most of her life, and publicly since 1982, when her first novel, *God Stalk*, was published.

Perhaps she has not achieved the acclaim and respect she deserves because, paradoxically, her Kencyrath world does not easily lend itself to external literary references the way a Tolkien does. Scholars love to find sources and precedents, like Icelandic Eddas or Celtic myths. Hodgell seems to create more from deep personal sources and keen observations of the world around her. Her imagination may have been fed by extensive reading and intimate familiarity with the engines of scholarship, but it is her keen eye for human behavior and her great understanding of human nature that informs her extensive cast of characters and the intricate complexity of their surroundings and situations. She is more intent on telling tales than inventing myths, though myths will emerge from the process. You can begin reading any one of her novels or stories and almost instantly you are drawn in. She always finds the little detail or the telling gesture that brings the simplest scenes to life.

And in her latest novel, *Deathless Gods*, you can find yourself recognizing contemporary concerns and attitudes in the midst of a world that otherwise seems so far away from our own, yet does so without conceding to giving characters contemporary idioms or attitudes.

The plot, as usual, is too dense to be summarized here with any justice, but be assured that Hodgell's storytelling skills will keep you from becoming lost.

There's been much talk of recent about how heroic fantasy is "fundamentally conservative": chaos comes to idyllic world, is struggled with by heroic types and finally conquered, returning the world to a status quo. Hodgell's novels have always put the lie to this oversimplification. Her Kencyrath world was never an idyll, and nothing ever remains stable there long enough to resemble a status quo. It may be far from the grim brutality of a George R. R. Martin, but it is a richer, more human, more *real* secondary world.

Hodgell deserves a much wider audience for her work.

◆◆◆

Penric's Labors
by Lois McMaster Bujold
Baen
November 2022
ISBN: 978-1-9821-9224-2

I usually don't review Lois McMaster Bujold books because, hey, if you don't know by now how good her work is on so many levels …

This book, however, seems a good place to start for uninitiated fantasy readers (science fiction readers will need to look elsewhere). Besides, it's not a novel, but three novellas, and they're not tied together like the old "fixups" of days of yore. I love novellas, and these especially.

This is the third collection (if I'm counting correctly) devoted to the sorcerer Learned Penric and his temple demon Desdemona. Penric may be no Miles Vorkosigan (but then who is?) but he is an affable, compelling, and fully engaging character. He doesn't hold a candle to Desdemona, though. The interplay between them would make enjoyable reading enough, but Bujold has engineered these three novellas with more than requisite thrills and wit. Each novella builds on the previous one to expand upon our understanding and appreciation of "Pen and Des" and their world. I can only imagine new readers becoming thoroughly captivated with her storytelling here.

And if they are, she has not only included an introduction, but an "outroduction" to help acquaint them with the World of the Five Gods. Add to that, for completists, she includes her own "Reading Order Guide" for anyone who wants to tackle the complete Bujold *oeuvre*. Of course, I disagree with it (my renegade suggestion is to begin with the brilliant standalone novel, *Falling Free*) but what do I know? I'm just the guy who always gets on the train at the wrong station. Better to get the word from the author herself. You won't be disappointed.

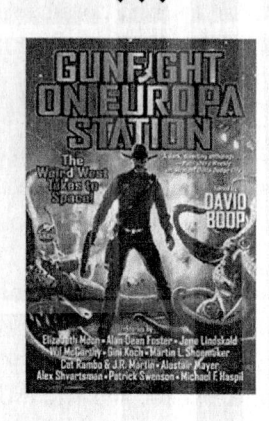

◆◆◆

Gunfight on Europa Station
edited by David Boop
Baen
November 2022 (mass market; first printing November 2021)
ISBN: 978-1-9821-9227-3

This is not my usual anthology and not my usual reading, but I enjoyed this for very personal reasons. Let me explain (but stop me if I go on).

I lost my mom last July. In her last few years, I'd visit her every Sunday. I'd bring burgers, and after we ate, we'd watch westerns on TV. She loved westerns, a taste she picked up from my grandfather. She loved every kind of western (except the boring ones that had too much talking).

One day, we couldn't find her western channel, and for some reason I flipped around the dial. We came upon an episode of *Star Trek* (the original series), and I kept it on to see if my mom might get interested.

After two minutes, my mom declared, "This is stupid!"

My mom hated science fiction. I changed the channel.

So, as I read through *Gunfight at Europa Station*, I kept wondering if one story or another might appeal to my mom, and in some small way help repair the rifts in our favored kinds of stories.

David Boop has gathered some fine work here. Funny, exciting, suspenseful, meditative—a great variety of styles and content. All good stuff. I'm especially fond of Boop's own contribution, "Last Stand at Europa Station A," and the stories by Elizabeth Moon, Jane Lindskold, Alan Dean Foster, Martin L. Shoemaker, and Alex Shvartsman. Also of note, as a special favorite, is the collaboration by Cat Rambo and J. R. Martin, "Riders of the Endless Void."

There's something here for everyone.

Except my mom.

Alas.

I'd like to hope I'm wrong. That somewhere out beyond the lone prairie, up where the Ghost Riders gallop, she'll find a story that brings together ten-gallon hats and space helmets, steeds and lightspeeds.

I miss watching those old shows with my mom—and miss my mom—but this book has been a great consolation.

❖ ❖ ❖

Sword and Planet
edited by Christopher Ruocchio
Baen
September 2022 (mass market; first printing December 2021)
ISBN: 978-1-9821-9214-3

I started teaching a science fiction litf class last fall. Better late than never. One of the things I've discovered is that a significant contingent of my students believe that the term "science fiction" is indistinguishable, nay synonymous, with "space opera." It has been my goal all term to disabuse them of this erroneous simplification.

However, if they're going to read space opera, or a brand of it that resembles heroic fantasy with warp drives, and a copy of the David Hartwell-Kathryn Cramer-edited *The Space Opera Renaissance* isn't handy, they can do worse than to dig into this compact and absorbing collection of original stories.

Yes, they are mashups of science and magic, but more often than not the science comes out on top, and in a satisfying (and often witty) way.

I try not to slight any contributors here, since it's all good work, including the editor's own contribution, "Queen Amid Ashes," but I was most drawn to "A Murder of Knights" by Tim Akers, "A Funny Thing Happened on the Way to Nakh-Maru" by Jessica Cluess, "The Fruits of Reputation" by Jody Lynn Nye, and "The Test" by T.C. McCarthy.

In fact, I think I'll gift my copy to one of my more worthy students at the end of the term. It may be "new stuff" that resembles the "old stuff," but this is the *good* new stuff, as they used to say.

The Dabare Snake Launcher
by Joelle Presby
Baen
November 2022
ISBN: 978-1-9821-9225-9

African themes, settings, and perspective have been showing up with greater frequency in contemporary science fiction. It's become much more than a novelty. It's a necessity. Cultural perspectives elsewhere on our planet have hit or are hitting something of a stasis. Africa, so far, has not yet had its turn. That science fiction writers in general would look there for new ideas and new possibilities seems more than likely. It's inevitable.

Joelle Presby's novel is about the construction and initial operation of the first space elevator, and it's located in west Africa. "Dabarre," we are told at the outset, is a Fulani term that means a piece of machinery fashioned from repurposed parts that either works perfectly—or not at all. So, some sense of the "stakes" is pretty clear as well. The voice and structure of the novel are fairly traditional, but it has a great cast of characters and is an exciting story, filled with all the wit and neat ideas we love to find in good science fiction. This novel left me feeling very optimistic. If not for the planet, then for the form of literature we love so much.

Copyright © 2023 by Richard Chwedyk.

Alan Smale is the double Sidewise Award-winning author of the Clash of Eagles trilogy, and his shorter fiction has appeared in Asimov's *and numerous other magazines and original anthologies. His latest novel,* Hot Moon, *came out last year from CAEZIK SF & Fantasy. When he is not busy creating wonderful new stories, he works as an astrophysicist and data archive manager at NASA's Goddard Space Flight Center.*

TURNING POINTS

by Alan Smale

X-RAY LASERS

Hey, does anyone remember Star Wars? No, not the movies. The other Star Wars, the Strategic Defense Initiative of the mid-1980s. If you don't, the idea was to develop a range of advanced weaponry to serve as a shield to protect us against incoming Soviet intercontinental ballistic missiles (ICBMs). Its ambitious agenda was to "[render] nuclear weapons impotent and obsolete (Ronald Reagan, March 23, 1983)—or at least the ones fired at the United States.

X-ray lasers were a key component of SDI. X-ray lasers, directed-energy weapons, fired from space-based platforms, to shoot down Soviet ICBMs as part of our anti-ballistic missile defense. The laser light would be generated by the detonation of a US nuclear weapon—yes, in space—that would (very briefly) energize dozens of directed X-ray lasers to take out a similar number of Soviet missiles at a stroke, at potential ranges of thousands of miles.

This was Project Excalibur, and it was … extremely technically demanding, to say the least. They'd have needed to power an array of maybe 50 X-ray laser rods, each three to ten feet long and each tracking a separate (and fast-moving) missile, detonate the conventional explosives to drive the fission necessary to set off the nuke, and then ensure that the bright X-ray pulse created would lase the rods, while each rod maintained a lock on its target.

That's a big ask. (Laser expert Jeff Hecht calls SDI "one of the wildest schemes ever pursued by the United States government.") The idea was also diplomatically dangerous, since testing the system would have required detonating nuclear weapons in orbit. Eventually, though, the technical difficulties proved insurmountable and Project Excalibur was canceled in 1992.

Of course, directed-energy weapons—lasers and phasers and ray-guns and all, have long been a staple of science fiction, and there are still plenty of military uses for lasers. But we're now entering an era where the peaceful application of high-powered X-ray lasers will have an astonishingly broad effect on just about every area of science you can think of—with countless knock-on effects on many areas of our everyday lives.

The 2018 Nobel Prize for Physics was awarded "for groundbreaking inventions in the field of laser physics" to Arthur Ashkin, Gerard Morou, and Donna Strickland. The Committee was commemorating advances in lasers that would allow "optical tweezers" to "grab" individual particles, atoms, and cells—literally using light to move the tiniest physical objects (Ashkin), and also create extremely short and intense laser pulses, known as "chirped pulse amplification" (CPA; Strickland and Morou). This may all sound obscure until I tell you that the winners did their original work back in the 1980s, and that CPA is the basis behind the corrective eye surgeries that millions of people receive each year.

(The Nobel Prize often has a really long fuse. Pun intended.)

So if that was the laser state of the art forty years ago, where are we now?

Well, on the brink of a revolution in physics, chemistry, biology, materials science, and many other areas, that's where.

Light is a big deal, obviously. Coherent light, that can be focused to a tight spot (spatial coherence) is an even bigger deal, and not just because you can use a laser pointer to drive your cat bonkers. Optical lasers big and small are used all over the place in the modern world: for surgery, for cutting and welding, for communications and in computers, in DNA sequencing and crystallography, in reading barcodes, in entertainment … lasers are everywhere. But there's even more they can do.

You see, lasers with high temporal coherence can either have an extremely narrow spectrum—the "pure" light at a single frequency that most people associate with lasers—

or a broader spectrum but an extremely short duration, down to a femtosecond—one millionth of a billionth of a second.

And why is that important? Because in one femtosecond, light travels about 0.3 micrometers, which is about the diameter of a virus. A femtosecond is also the timescale of some chemical reactions, and of atomic motion; it's the timescale for an atomic electron to "orbit" its nucleus. That's some super-small stuff that scientists would like to get a really good look at, but haven't been able to until recently.

Say hello to the XFEL: the X-ray Free-electron Laser.

We've known since the 1970s that electron beams passing through a periodic electric or magnetic field can stimulate X-ray emission, and that those X-rays might power lasers, but it's really only been in the past couple of decades that free-electron X-ray lasers have really come into their own. The first was a laser called FLASH, at the Deutsches Elektronen-Synchrotron (DESY) in Hamburg, Germany, in 2005. Next came the Linac Coherent Light Source (LCLS), which saw first light in 2009 at the Stanford Linear Accelerator Center (SLAC). In its first ten years of operation, 900 experiments performed at LCLS produced 1300 scientific papers. Both facilities are still going strong, and have been joined by SACLA (Japan, 2011), FERMI (Italy, 2014), PAL-XFEL (South Korea, 2017), DCLS VUV FEL (China, 2017), and Swiss FEL (2019), with several more soon to become operational.

With these machines, scientists can study the structure of proteins and enzymes, the transition states of many chemical reactions, nanoscale dynamics and other ultrafast phenomena. You can guess that these lasers are a bit bigger than the one in your

Blu-Ray player. The electron accelerators used in the current fourth-generation XFELs are kilometer-sized, and the undulators (the mechanism used for the radiation generation) are hundred-meter-sized. They're billion-dollar investments at the national and international scale, requiring decades to build, and they're extremely oversubscribed: only a small fraction of proposed experiments can be performed. It's also pretty rare to repeat an experiment, even though many science topics require a lot of data of different types to study properly.

Nonetheless, discoveries made using XFELS have already provided insights into the development of new drugs, and in helping to understand how existing medications act within the human body at a fundamental level. Scientists have studied the function of natural toxins to kill mosquito larvae that carry malaria and West Nile virus, raising the possibility of extending them to combat Zika virus and dengue fever. They've probed the physics of plasmas at astronomical temperatures and densities. The range of discoveries just in biophysics and crystallography has filled several books.

But the next step is—you guessed it—the fifth-generation XFEL, and it's just around the corner. This is where XFELS go from megafacilities to tabletop machines, with their price falling to the point where every university, hospital, and independent lab can afford them—and will buy them.

How? Well, we're talking cutting-edge tech now, but here's some jargon for your next nerd cocktail party: the fifth generation of X-ray lasers will be based on laser-wakefield accelerators, driven by powerful deep-infrared lasers, driving undulators that will push the beam above the X-ray lasing threshold. All at a tiny fraction of the cost of a linear accelerator, maybe tens of thousands of dollars per rig, rather than billions. There's also the prospect of driving the pulse lengths down to the attosecond level—a thousand times shorter than a femtosecond.

Phew. Got all that? Now you know.

And that's where the science avalanche really begins, because hundreds, eventually thousands of separate research teams will be able to perform years-worth of experiments in their own dedicated areas of expertise.

Scientists will directly image matter at subatomic spatial scales, and make movies of the evolving dynamics of super-short chemical and physical reactions. They'll study coherent electron and ion motion within molecules, and the transfer of charge across solid-state junctions and biological membranes, all separated out by the individual elements involved. There are many quantum level transient-state processes in biology and materials science that we have no real understanding of. Now, we'll achieve that understanding.

This isn't just abstract geekery. The findings will lead to improvements in batteries, solar cells, and bioenergy; firm up the strength and reliability of everything from bridges to airplane avionics; and decode intercellular communication to help us combat viruses and communicable disease. Examining the very small can also tell us about the very large: we'll be able to study the plasma physics of tiny amounts of matter under the extreme pressures that create both heavy elements and planetary bodies. Studies of nonequilibrium states in the quantum vacuum will have implications for cosmology.

My examples here are just scratching the surface, but in short: we can't fail to make rapid leaps in vacuum quantum dynamics, medicine, semiconductors, catalytic chemistry, biosystems, aerosols, and plasma physics. The discoveries will usher in a slew of next-generation pharmaceuticals, materials, and electronics. We'll see improved health, better energy efficiency, cooler devices, and maybe a cooler planet.

We'll also find some surprises, I'm sure. We'll need to be ready for the unexpected.

All of this won't happen tomorrow. There's still work to be done. Science takes time. But it's clear that the coming decade will see a flood of new science with immediate real-world applications.

An explosion of illuminating breakthroughs, if you will, with X-ray lasers at the center, and beneficial spinoffs shooting out in all directions.

And this is just one of several turning points in science and technology that we're right in the middle of. More on some others in future columns.

Copyright © 2023 by Alan Smale.

New York Times *and* USA Today *bestselling L. Penelope is the award-winning author of* the Earthsinger Chronicles *and* The Monsters We Defy. *Her first novel,* Song of Blood & Stone, *was chosen as one of* TIME *Magazine's 100 Best Fantasy Books of All Time. Equally left and right-brained, she studied filmmaking and computer science in college and sometimes dreams in HTML. She hosts the* My Imaginary Friends *podcast and lives in Maryland with her husband and furry dependents. Visit her at: http://www.lpenelope.com*

LONGHAND

by L. Penelope

12 TIPS FOR BEATING WRITER'S BLOCK

Writer's block is like the boogeyman lurking under the beds and in the shadowy closets of every writer. Some are plagued by terror of its presence. Others claim not to believe in it at all. But just about every writer I know has experienced periods where the words just wouldn't come. Whether it's not knowing the story you want to tell, not wanting to write the story you're supposed to, or being in the middle of something that just feels wrong and you can't move forward until it starts feeling right again, the condition takes many forms.

I've been infected by it more times than I can count. In fact, I was stuck on my current work-in-progress for the past few weeks and am just now recovering my flow and pace. What went wrong? I had a full outline for the novel, which is book two in a trilogy. I knew the broad strokes of where the story needs to end in order to set up for the next book. I had the main characters living in my head, both of whom appeared in the first book. I'd already re-written the first twenty-thousand words of the draft once, but for the longest time I just couldn't get out of the first act of the novel.

This is not the first time this has happened. In fact, if I didn't get stuck at some point (or multiple points) in a manuscript, that would be far more noteworthy. So, since I've been through this a time or twelve and have always gotten out of it (even if while I'm mired in it, it feels like I'll never break free) I've developed some tools for chipping away at the dreaded block. Here are my twelve tips for getting unstuck.

1. Re-read what you've written.

This assumes you're not stuck on the first page, which I admit has never happened to me. No matter how much I've written, revisiting it is always the first step. Try looking at the words you have with a critical eye. What are they accomplishing? How is the setup of the story? The rising action? The characterization? Is there something here that you've gotten wrong and is holding up your further progress?

2. Talk it out with someone.

Whether it's a critique partner, a non-writer friend, or family member, talk through the story with another human being. Describing the story you have, the story you want, and what feels wrong about where you are now can often jog something inside you. And your listener may have suggestions that, while not necessarily correct, also spark an idea that could get you back on track.

3. Put it through a (different) plotting system.

This one is for the plotters. I usually start with one or two plotting systems when I initially outline my books. Then, when I'm stuck, I pull out a third or fourth one and plot out my beats. Looking at it from a different perspective can often put the problem into better focus.

4. Break down all the actions necessary to resolve the plot problem.

I like to use the 8 essential story points from the Dramatica story development theory for this. In brief, these are: the goal of the story; the requirements for achieving the goal; the consequences if the goal isn't met; the forewarnings that suggesting the consequences are getting closer; the dividends or small rewards resulting from seeking the goal; the costs of pursuing the goal; the prerequisites for the requirements; and the preconditions or small plot obstacles leading to the forewarnings. Breaking the big story into all the tiny pieces gives me ideas for scenes and conflicts to write or a hint as to what I'm missing.

5. **Complete a character profile.**

Most of the time, my story problems go back to my characters and me not knowing them well enough to write them organically. Revisiting their goals and motivations, their backstories, emotional wounds and flaws helps me to get inside their heads more and write their actions and reactions from a more motivated place.

6. **Brainstorm in a different medium.**

Often my brainstorming is on the computer, typing notes into a text file. However, when I'm stuck, I try to change it up. I will write by hand in my notebook or on a tablet. Or use voice memos to talk it out to myself. Or, if I stay on the computer, use a different font or color to change the way I look at my notes and ideas.

7. **Write potential scenes on notecards.**

Notecards have a kind of impermanence to them which is helpful when I'm stuck. I will grab a stack and a Sharpie and just put all my ideas for potential scenes, conflicts, and character behaviors on a bunch of cards just to get them out of my head. Anything that could possibly happen in the story goes on a card. Some will get tossed out, but some will inevitably make their way into the story.

8. **Do a backwards outline and start from the end.**

Stories are about cause and effect, and if you're a writer who knows what the end is up front, then start there and work backwards. How does the heroine defeat the antagonist? What happens just before that which gives her the final things she needs for the victory? What happens just before that? Each element of the story is a link in the chain and coming at it from the end can give you an idea of the logical prior steps.

9. **Detail character GMC. Are the goals in conflict?**

GMC or goal, conflict, and motivation, are some of the first essential building blocks of story that I learned. Vibrant, active characters need to be trying to achieve something and facing obstacles along the way. Detailing what they want, why they want it, and what is stopping them from achieving it are the strong foundations of successful stories. And if your protagonist and antagonist have goals which conflict, even better.

10. **Fill the well.**

Sometimes we just need inspiration and to rest and reset our brains. The creative well can feel all dried up when the words aren't flowing. Refill yours by watching a favorite movie, re-reading a favorite book, or checking out something brand new. You don't have to read a master work to inspire you, though you certainly could. Even a novel or story you don't particularly like can at least give you the confidence that you could do better. But if it does speak to something inside you, use that as fuel for your personal fire.

11. **Step away from the computer. Touch grass. Take a walk. Get some vitamin D.**

That's it, that's the tip.

12. **But always show up again.**

At the end of the day, I always get unstuck because I keep at it until I do. I don't give up, and I don't stop writing. I show up at my desk with regularity, keeping the appointment I make with myself to prioritize my writing even when it's hard (especially when it's hard).

I know the title says there are twelve tips, but here are a few more, just for fun. Find one of the many worldbuilding questionnaires or checklists available online and answer some questions. Do a tarot pull or use a deck of specialized story inspiration cards like the Story Engine or Story Forge

Write a backstory scene that won't be in the book. Write the book's blurb or back cover copy. Write a paragraph about why you wanted to write this story in the first place—what was the initial idea that captured your attention? Revisit the theme of the story, or brainstorm to figure out the theme if you don't know what it is yet. Write a positive review of the finished story—what you hope someone would say about it. Retype a short story from a favorite author and notice how they put their words and ideas together.

Getting stuck or blocked is just a part of the writer's life, and though it may feel like a catastrophe, it doesn't have to be. You can develop a toolbox of ideas to have on hand that will help you feel confident the block will end. Then all you have to do is keep calm and write on.

Copyright © 2023 by L. Penelope.

author Kristine Kathryn Rusch writes in almost every genre. Generally, she uses her real name (Rusch) for most of her writing. Under that name, she publishes bestselling science fiction and fantasy (including the Fey series, the Retrieval Artist series and the Diving series), award-winning mysteries, acclaimed mainstream fiction, controversial nonfiction, and the occasional romance. Her novels have made bestseller lists around the world and her short fiction has appeared in more than twenty best of the year collectiowww.ns. She has won more than twenty-five awards for her fiction, including the Hugo, Le Prix Imaginales, the Asimov's Readers Choice award, and the Ellery Queen Mystery Magazine Readers Choice Award.

THE REFLECTION ON MOUNT VITAKI (PART II)

by Kristine Kathryn Rusch

THREE

They pounded three of the bolts in the middle of the area that Zed called the runway. It had the most wheel prints from his landings, and the least amount of dirt. It was also far away from the edges, so they wouldn't easily trigger any slides.

Matvei believed that pounding something into the dirt anywhere on top of this peak would start slides, but he had no facts to base that opinion on. He was also going by hunches, which made Kyra both annoyed and feel better. Because no one knew what was going on up here, everyone was reverting to behaviors she hadn't seen in a long time from these people, if ever.

And herself. She couldn't forget herself.

As they assembled the pulley system, which could be used with and without the bolts (if they broke off or got too wobbly), she made herself focus on the effort. Assembling a pulley was second nature to all of them. Each one of them had done so in the middle of an emergency, when another climber had been unable to pull themselves back up to the group.

The pulleys were designed to handle human weight, even under the most difficult of circumstances, which Kyra hoped they would not experience here.

Zed made them promise that when they finished, they would pull the bolts from the ground, so that he had the full range of the mountain peak if the demiglider needed it.

Kyra had agreed. If she came back for a second time after her trip down the side of the mountain, she would make sure she had different equipment. The bolts and pulleys were built for the mountains, but they weren't the best system for a complex series of climbs. The systems that were the best were hugely expensive.

Once the pulley system was assembled, Kyra double-checked the ropes for breaks, cuts, or burns. Then she inspected the levers and the flywheels. Last, she looked at the bolts. Those were the most mysterious part. They might've been weakened by the weather, but she couldn't tell just by eyeballing them.

Neither could anyone else, and they all checked.

The weather had gotten warmer as the sun became more intense. Warmer was a relative thing, though. Now, she didn't feel like her skin would seize up from the cold. Now, she was just chilly.

She knew that would disappear once she started down the mountain face.

Before they even started putting on their equipment, Kyra had given Alyoshi the chance to back out. He had been so negative all morning that she didn't want him to go if he was terrified. He wasn't that much lighter than Matvei or Uliana.

But Alyoshi insisted on going, and she had a hunch part of his reason was to keep an eye on her.

They tightened their clothes, then stepped into the special harness, with the ropes already in place. The belay tubes on both harnesses were made of mountainstone, as tradition required. Centuries of climbs and rappels had shown that belay tubes, made from the actual mountains themselves, gave the devices an additional, measurable strength.

Since Kyra was not an engineer, she had no idea why that was. But she had to trust them on this, as in all things.

Then she and Alyoshi double-checked their snacks and water containers. She hated the added weight, but there was no choice.

Then, with one final check, she and Alyoshi walked in tandem to the edge of the peak. He did not look down, and this time, neither did she.

They waited, though, just to see if the edge would hold their combined weight.

It did.

Kyra looked at Alyoshi. She didn't ask him if he was ready, like she usually would have. She didn't want him to back out of the trip.

She made a small circular gesture with her right index finger. Alyoshi sighed as he saw it, but followed the silent command.

He turned his back on the edge of the mountain. So did Kyra.

The rest of her team stood near the bolts. Kyra had supervised setting up the ropes, anchoring them properly to the bolts, along with her favorite devices to feed the ropes through the openings in the bolts. But she was happy to have people back there, to take control should something go very wrong.

Uliana stood in the center as if she expected to have to take charge. She probably would have to, given Zed's lack of experience with this part of the trip, and Matvei's surprising attitude problem.

But they looked as prepared as they could be.

"All right," Kyra said to Alyoshi. "Let's go."

His mouth moved. He said, "Yeah," but so softly that she couldn't really hear him. The wind teased his hair, but she couldn't feel any wind at all.

She pulled her ropes tightly, concentrating on her right hand—her brake hand—making sure that her gloves were thick enough to handle this should something go wrong.

Then she glanced over her shoulder at the edge, but managed not to look down.

The clouds were closer than they had been a moment before, almost like they were spotting her, or threatening to move in should she do anything wrong.

She leaned back in her harness, resting her butt against the equipment as if she was sitting on a chair. The last test, making sure it could handle her weight.

She hadn't been too concerned about it because she had double-checked everything. Her harness was good. So was Alyoshi's.

He mimicked her movement.

They hovered over the edge of the mountain, feet against the lip, for just a moment, before she began lowering.

She used her left hand—her guide hand—to ease herself down, feet against the mountainside. Her climbing shoes, designed to grip everything, had trouble finding purchase on the smooth surface, just like she expected.

That didn't stop her stomach from taking a small leap of its own. She usually didn't have nerves, but she had them this morning, because everything was unfamiliar, and it felt like the entire world was at stake.

She had to clear that expectation from her mind. The entire world was *not* at stake. If this didn't work, her life would not change.

But if it did work, as Magnus had predicted, then everything would be different.

She made herself concentrate on the descent. She leaned back slightly, keeping her toes against that smooth surface. Her legs were perpendicular to the mountain, the only part of this she really didn't have to think about.

That position was as natural as walking for her, because she had done it so often. And it was easier when the mountainside was smooth than when it jutted out at all angles.

Maybe that was the only benefit to this weird mountain—the predictable angle of its decline. She kept looking from side to side to make sure nothing was falling toward them or that she or Alyoshi had loosened something on the mountainside.

Alyoshi should have been doing the same, but he seemed to be having some trouble. He was only a few yards from her, but it seemed like he was on a different mountain altogether.

The muscles in his arms bulged. He was hanging on tightly. The wind kept moving his hair and, she realized, also trying to push him away from the mountain. When that didn't seem to work, it was trying to slam him into the mountain.

No wind bothered her at all, which was odd, because there were no natural barriers between them. He must have been rappelling down some kind of wind tunnel, some weird air current was catching him while avoiding her altogether.

As he moved his head, his gaze caught hers. She pointed up, knowing he wouldn't be able to hear her, even if she shouted.

But he should understand the gesture.

Did you want to go back?

She wasn't entirely clear, though. She wasn't asking if *they* should go back. Just if *he* wanted to.

He shook his head, then glanced downward, as if searching for another spot to place his feet. He almost never did that. Or maybe, he was just looking to see how far they had to go.

She wasn't going to let herself do that. She was going down bit by bit, measuring her pace the way she always did. She had learned to do so by counting the seconds between pushing back ever so slightly, and then moving forward.

Only she didn't really push back here. There wasn't much to measure against. It was easier—and better—to keep her feet on the mountainside, once she had found real purchase with her shoes.

Alyoshi was trying to push and pull himself, and it wasn't working. The wind was tangling his ropes, blowing his hair in his face, shoving him in different directions.

He had to hold tight to keep from slamming against the mountain.

She was about to tell him to go back up, when her feet hit air.

She looked down. What seemed like part of the rock face was actually a dark opening.

Then she looked up. She had gone faster than she'd expected to, maybe because she hadn't been fighting the geography of the mountainside.

She had reached the location of the reflection point.

She eased herself downward a little slower, because her feet were dangling now.

Alyoshi was near her, but he was swinging on his ropes, almost out of control in that wind. Now, it was blowing him backwards. Where her feet were dangling, his were being pushed underneath him, hurting his form.

She pointed up insistently with her guide hand, but he shook his head.

He clearly wasn't going to leave unless she did.

Besides, they appeared to have arrived.

She slid down farther on the rope, using more control than she had before, because her feet were dangling. When her head finally cleared that lip, she blinked in surprise.

A cave greeted her.

Its top was as smooth as the side of the mountain. The top of the cave was an arch that extended as far as she could see.

She tried not to shift with excitement, but she had never felt this way—almost breathless with anticipation.

She wasn't sure what she had expected, but it hadn't been a cave.

She lowered just a bit more, to try to see deeper into the darkness, but she couldn't.

The air was still here, and smelled faintly perfumed as if there was an unfamiliar incense burning inside.

She wanted to keep going, to see how far this went, but she was supposed to wait for Alyoshi. He was still struggling with that weird wind current, fighting his way down as if each drop was a victory.

He would be exhausted when they got ready to ascend. She would tell him to use the sign to encourage the team at the top to essentially pull him up.

She hoped he would listen.

She was dangling in the still air. She hated it. So she looked down, trying to see where the bottom of the cave opening was to see if she could brace her feet on it.

As she twisted, she gasped with surprise. There wasn't a lip at the bottom of the cave opening. There was an entire platform—flat and perfect.

She could rest there and wait for him.

She slowly eased down. The cave mouth was much larger than she expected—maybe thirty feet high and just as wide.

The interior of the cave was extremely dark, which also surprised her. She had thought, from down below, that perhaps there was something that would reflect the sun on this part of the mountain, a clear section or maybe just the angle of the mountainside.

She hadn't expected a cave. That seemed almost counterintuitive. There was nothing to reflect.

She glanced up. Alyoshi was struggling not to get tangled in his ropes, like a beginning climber. He wasn't even looking at her. He had to concentrate on what he was doing.

She eased the rest of the way down, then pushed away from the edge, so that she wouldn't stop on that platform. If she and Alyoshi were working in tandem, one of them would have gone farther down while the other stopped on the platform.

But they weren't. He was still far above her.

So she checked first.

She didn't really go below the platform, but she went far enough that she could see what was underneath it. That way, she wouldn't have to change her configuration at all, from descent to ascent. Doing that would have taken more time than she wanted.

She kept her feet braced on the edge of the platform and peered over the side. The platform had been carved into the mountainside. The brown-black smoothness continued beneath the platform as if the cave didn't exist at all.

So, unless there was some kind of gaping hole underneath the platform that she couldn't see, the platform was secure.

She leaned forward even more and balanced on her toes, then pulled herself up just slightly. She shuffled her feet inward until they were flat on the platform and then she stood, slowly, putting all her weight on her feet.

The platform shifted ever so slightly, making her gasp. Then a bright white light appeared inside the cave. Her heart pounded. She hadn't expected a light. Was that what the sun caught? Whatever caused the light?

Or was it a whoever? And if it was, how could it be a person? How would they have gotten here?

She looked up.

Alyoshi was clinging to his ropes with all of his strength, twisting in what looked like a gale, a gale she couldn't feel at all.

He had made it far enough down that she could reach him. She grabbed his ankles and stabilized him.

There was no wind. None. She had no idea why he was twisting like that.

He glanced down at her in surprise. He hadn't realized she was so close.

His entire body was trembling.

"How are you there?" he asked.

"There's a platform," she said.

"Where?" he asked.

His face was chapped and red. It certainly looked like he had windburn.

"Right beneath me," she said. She didn't ask why he wasn't seeing anything because she had no idea if the wind had covered his eyes in dust and debris. She'd had that experience. It was deeply unpleasant.

"I don't see it," he said, sounding almost panicked. Alyoshi never panicked. That was one of the things she liked most about him.

Yet this entire trip had put him on edge and had made him into someone she didn't recognize.

"Let me guide you," she said, gently pulling him downward, careful not to upset the delicate balance he had made with the ropes.

His body was trembling, a sign of just how much energy he had been using. She hoped he would have enough strength to make it all the way back to the top.

He scrabbled with his feet as if they couldn't find the platform at all. She had to hold him in place to get his feet onto the platform, but he didn't seem to trust it.

Finally, he seemed to catch his balance. He stood, gingerly, but clung to his ropes as if he was afraid to let them go.

"What the hell is here?" he asked, blinking at her.

The light coming from inside the cave did not illuminate his face, which she found very strange. Every time she moved even slightly away from him, the wind started back up—at least around him—messing his hair, playing with the edges of his clothing.

"A cave," she said. "It goes really deep. And warm air is blowing out of the entrance."

"Where?" he asked.

"There," she said, trying not to sound as confused as she felt. "Where that light is coming from. Come closer, so you can feel the warmth."

"I don't see a light," he said.

She extended a hand, pointing into the cave itself.

"Okay, that's strange," he said. Then, gingerly, he extended his guide hand and it seemed to hit something solid. "This is just an indent in the rock. Not a cave."

"It's a cave." She put her hand next to his, but there was nothing solid near her fingers or her palm. Her hand went as far forward as it had before.

He looked at her with something like fright.

"This makes no sense, Kyra," he said. "Am I hallucinating?"

Or was she? It was a valid question, in the thin air.

"What do you see when you look at my hand?" she asked him.

"That it goes much farther forward than mine," he said. "But I'm hitting solid rock."

She threaded her fingers with his and then extended their hands forward, past the point where his had gotten blocked.

"Okay," he said, still sounding scared. "I'm seeing our hands go through solid rock and disappearing."

Something was really wrong. He sounded convinced of what he saw, but it wasn't what was there.

She glanced up. The team was there, and he would need help getting back.

This climb was over, even though she didn't want it to be.

"Let me do one thing," she said. "Stay here, where it's warm."

He frowned at her—at least, she thought that was a frown. But she wasn't going to let it stop her.

This might be the only chance she ever got to see inside that cave.

She reached into her pack and pulled out her spyglass. She put it to her eye and peered as far from that light as she could.

But the light kept catching her. It came out of a vase, which sat on a table. It almost looked like the vase contained and controlled the light.

The table was long and clearly carved out of the mountainside. The table stood freely in the center of the cave's main room. Behind it, she thought she saw a fountain spewing water that reflected gold and white as the drops sailed through the air.

She turned away from the light and blinked. It took a moment for her eyes to adjust. Then she saw shelves and tables outlined against the darkness of the rest of the cave. The shelves and tables were covered with all kinds of devices—some she recognized, like compasses and telescopes and lanterns, but others she only had a vague sense of.

"Kyra." Alyoshi's voice trembled.

She had to take care of him. He was her top priority now. She would do so in a moment, but she just wanted to see as much as she could.

She swung the spyglass to the other side and was surprised to see a harpsichord with a lute resting on its bench. Other instruments hung nearby—on the cave wall? On shelves? It was too dark to tell.

She saw the outlines of mandolins and crumhorns and natural horns and recorders. On one side were trumpets and bugles and circular horns. Beyond them, globes and maybe maps and perhaps still cameras like the ones that gave her fits in her work.

She wished she had them now. Even though it took forever to create an image, and even though the light was probably poor here, she would be able to prove to the others that this cave was worth exploring.

Kyra turned toward Alyoshi and was about to hand him the spyglass, so he could confirm what she had seen when she actually looked at him.

Frost covered his eyebrows and eyelashes. His eyes were barely open, and he was shivering so badly that he looked like he would shake off his harness.

She wasn't even sure if he could see her anymore. "Alyoshi!" she said. He blinked toward her. His hands looked frozen to his ropes, which was both good and bad. He wasn't falling backwards, but he wouldn't be able to help them pull him up.

Saving him was definitely on her now.

She reached into her kit and found more rope, tying him into the harness according to the protocol. Then she grabbed his guiding hand. It seemed to have frozen to his lead rope.

Her hands were frost free. She wasn't even cold. The air coming from inside that cave was warming her.

But whenever she touched Alyoshi, she felt the chill of the wind—almost like a hint of wind, as if it were blowing through a badly sealed window.

She had been about to ask him if he could help with his ascent at all, when his eyes closed. That sent a stab of fear through her.

He didn't have a lot of time left.

She unhooked his braking hand so that it wouldn't get tangled in the ropes and attached him to the harness as best she could.

She would have to follow him up, using the procedure for unconscious climbers.

Before she alerted the others to pull him up, she used the climber's code, tugging the message for *unconscious climber*. Both Uliana and Matvei would know what to do.

Then she tugged three times on Alyoshi's ropes and waited for a response.

She got it, along with an acknowledgment through her ropes that she would be handling the climb.

She let out a breath of air, marveling that she could see Alyoshi's breath, but not her own. It was as if she were indoors and he was out, even though there was nothing between them, no glass, no wall, no barrier of any kind.

The warm air from the cave enveloped her and protected her, kept her hands from shaking. The clouds still threatened off the sides of the mountain, but they seemed closer to Alyoshi than they were to her.

If only she could go inside the cave and wait. She could explore and see what all that equipment was. She could figure out the source of the warmth. She could—

Something tugged on her rope, catching her attention. It was a query.

Are you all right?

She must have waited too long between her communications.

Yes, she communicated in return. *One moment.*

There wasn't a lot of nuance in the climbing communications. She couldn't say that she still had to get Alyoshi ready or prepare herself. She couldn't apologize for lost time or try to explain the weird differences in the weather near the cave's mouth.

She couldn't think about any of that at the moment. She tucked Alyoshi's cold hands on his lap, made sure he was as stable as he could be, and then tugged the *lift* message on his rope.

It took a moment before she got an affirmative response on her ropes. By then, she had double-checked Alyoshi's position and double-checked her harness and ropes.

Unlike his, hers had no ice, no frost, and no problems. His looked like he'd been in deep snow. He was turning in the wind, the wind she couldn't feel, the wind that there was no evidence of on her side at all.

She couldn't think about that right now.

She eased herself over the side so she could assume the correct position—sitting in the harness, feet braced against the lip of the platform, legs perpendicular with the rock face—and then she sent the *lift me* tug.

That would activate everything—her rise alongside Alyoshi's. They would lift her a little slower than him, so that she would be slightly below him—but not on the same path. If he tumbled out of his harness—and people had—he would fall freely, without hitting her as he tumbled downward.

Her mouth went dry. She hadn't thought of all the things that could go wrong, not since she found the cave. The warmth no longer touched her, and the light seemed to have faded, although it left a ghost of itself whenever she closed her eyes.

She was just beginning to wonder what was going wrong, why hadn't they started pulling Alyoshi upwards, when he started to move. His legs dangled freely and his head bobbed.

He was completely unconscious.

His harness rose maybe two feet higher than hers when the team up above started to lift her.

She could help. She had reset her belay tube so that it acted more like a pulley. She hadn't done that on Alyoshi's, because to use the belay tube that way required the climber to be conscious and to know how to reverse the work they had done to get down.

Because she had the belay tube in place, her ascent was smoother than Alyoshi's. He bobbed and toppled from one side to another. The ropes jerked, and more than once, she thought he was going to fall.

She couldn't catch him, but she could maneuver herself to prop him up if she had to.

She was hoping she wouldn't have to. She'd done that on one climb, and it had been the most dangerous climb she had ever gone on. It had been a miracle that both of them survived.

Here, the distance wasn't as vast as that long-ago climb, but she still wasn't sure if Alyoshi was going to make it. The frost still coated his face and clothing. His legs dangled and his ropes still twisted.

Once he got well above the mouth of the cave, the winds seemed to die down. He still swung from side to side, but not as badly. The farther up he got, the less the wind seemed to be a factor.

As Kyra worked her way up, she didn't feel any wind at all. The air had gotten cooler, but that was only because the warm breeze from inside the cave had vanished.

She didn't understand what had happened on this trip. That would be something she would have to discuss with some scientists who specialized in wind or air currents or mountains. She had no idea what would cause one area of a mountainside to be completely calm while a nearby section would be buffeted by severe winds, particularly when the mountainside was as smooth as this one.

As she did half the work to pull herself up—figuring the team above had too much to do with Alyoshi—she focused on the wind and the science of air currents. She didn't want to think about what was happening with Alyoshi, nor did she want to think about what she had seen inside that cave.

It looked like strange treasure, a mishmash of things that she would never have placed together.

It implied that someone watched over the cave, kept an eye on it, maybe even used it.

But that implication might have been wrong, simply because what she saw made no real sense.

None of the items looked very old and yet some of them had to be. Many of them weren't being made any longer.

There was no obvious way for a person to get into the cave, not without climbing down to it or up to it, so by rights, those items should have been covered with spiderwebs and dust.

Maybe someone lived there, deep inside the bowels of that cave. Maybe that was why warm air escaped. Maybe there was some kind of heating—a furnace of some kind, using rocks from the mountain itself to fire up parts of the furnace. Or oil or some other precious substance that would burn and keep an enclosed space like that warm.

She didn't know, but she wanted to find out.

She let out a breath. She had promised herself she wouldn't think about any of that, and there she was, thinking about it, instead of paying attention to what was happening with Alyoshi.

He was tipped slightly backwards. One hand had fallen outside the ropes and dangled just like his feet.

If Alyoshi still had a long distance to go, Kyra would have hurried to catch up to him, sent a signal that she was moving closer to him, and take the risk of grabbing him and guiding him up.

But he was only about 50 feet from the top. Soon, she would see someone from her team leaning over and trying to ease him up.

And sure enough, just as she had that thought, Uliana's head peeked over the edge, concern on her face.

Kyra waved as a way of reassuring Uliana that Kyra was all right. And then she pointed at Alyoshi.

Uliana nodded, but didn't give Kyra any other acknowledgment.

If anything, Uliana's expression grew even more grim. She pushed away from the edge, which surprised Kyra. Kyra had expected her to reach down and help Alyoshi make that last distance.

Kyra's heart started to pound. The situation seemed to be worse than she thought. She had no idea what was going on, and she needed to.

Her feet were braced against the smooth side of the mountain. She had been pulling herself up slowly, without putting in as much effort from her legs as she could have.

Now she added them, pushing herself upwards, even though she was beginning to feel fatigued.

Alyoshi dangled and twisted. His head lolled.

Zed peered over the edge, a deep frown on his face. Uliana appeared beside him. She was saying something to him, and he was nodding, butKyra couldn't hear any of it.

They were laying on their stomachs, which gave them some leverage. Then Uliana looked at Kyra, and mimed *Stop*.

Finally, what they were doing made sense. They were going to concentrate all of their efforts on getting Alyoshi to the top and then they would worry about Kyra.

She nodded, and rested the toes of her boots against the mountain, hoping that would hold her enough.

Her upward movement had ceased. She wasn't happy with the position. She couldn't quite see what they were doing to get Alyoshi to the top. What she could see was a lot of movement—Uliana leaning, then disappearing, arms bracing, Zed turning slightly, Alyoshi spinning yet again.

Kyra's breath caught in her throat. Her team was so good at climbing and doing—well, most everything that it did—that she was no longer used to crises on important events.

She had known this would be hard. She just hadn't realized how dangerous it would be.

Waiting was not that good for her either. She hadn't realized how tired the ascent had made her. Her arms ached, and her feet were in an awkward position. There was still no wind here, but the clouds were getting closer.

Now, on top of everything else, she was worried about getting the demiglider off the mountain.

First things first, they had to get Alyoshi to safety. And then her.

Finally, Alyoshi's harness rose above the edge of the peak. Uliana and Zed dragged him toward them until Kyra could no longer see his legs or his boots.

He hadn't helped at all. She had held onto a small hope that he was injured or barely conscious and somehow able to assist with climbing over the edge. But he didn't. He had to be dragged.

She made herself release a small breath. She couldn't make up anything. It wouldn't help her.

Not that she was panicked. She wasn't. But she wasn't calm either. Things simply had not gone as planned.

She resisted the urge to glance over her shoulder to look down at the cave opening. Perhaps that had been the most surprising thing of all. She was still drawn to it. She wanted to solve all of its mysteries—and part of her was deeply annoyed that Alyoshi had gotten hurt somehow. Because that would slow her down. She would have to deal with his injuries and the perceptions of danger those injuries would bring.

Then she raised her eyebrows, feeling odd. That last thought was not charitable of her. Was she that selfish, that she worried more about what would happen because of Alyoshi's injuries than with the injuries themselves?

That didn't seem like her, and yet that was how she was feeling.

She made herself grip the ropes tighter, adjust her feet a little, and breathe the thin air. The morning had been surprising and upsetting. She needed to acknowledge that and move forward, whatever that meant.

She would think about the cave and its contents later. She would think about the future later. Right now, she had to get to the top of the mountain and get her team off of it.

At that thought, the signal came through her ropes. The team was going to help her the last of the way.

She adjusted her position one more time, then shot a glance at the clouds. They looked even darker and thicker than they had before.

But sunlight covered her, almost like a halo of warmth. She was grateful for it.

She braced her toes, rose up ever so slightly, and leaned into the pull as the team above worked the ropes.

She didn't have far to go. And even though she felt every ache in every muscle while she waited, the wait had benefited her. She had rested enough that she could put extra energy into getting to that mountain peak.

Or maybe her underlying worry fueled her. But she toed the smooth side of the mountain, used her arms as best she could, and finally her head rose above the lip.

She could see Matvei and Uliana working the ropes. Zed wasn't visible at all, and neither was Alyoshi, although his harness lay on the ground like the abandoned skin of a snake.

Kyra pulled herself the rest of the way, until her feet found the top. She walked forward, still hunched, and slowly stood when she reached the area that seemed far enough away from that edge.

She used the flat of her hand to tell Matvei and Uliana to stop pulling on the ropes. The ropes fell beside Kyra's boots.

Her guide hand still held the ropes, but her brake hand cramped. Her back ached, and her shoulders were on fire from the effort.

The clouds seemed to have moved even closer to the edge of the mountain. Darkness surrounded everything except the peak itself.

Kyra undid her harness and stepped out of it. The air was colder here than it was on the mountainside, and now—finally—a breeze caressed her cheeks.

The sunlight was fading—not because it was late (it wasn't), but because the clouds were rolling in, like big waves of fog.

Uliana hurried toward her. Matvei was running toward the demiglider.

"Where's Alyoshi?" Kyra asked, when Uliana reached her side.

"Are you all right?" Uliana asked, ignoring her question.

"Exhausted, but all right," Kyra said.

"You're not cold?" Uliana asked. She seemed confused.

"There was a cave down there. I was on the platform. There was warm air coming from inside. I tried to get Alyoshi to the same place, but I couldn't. He never seemed to feel the warmth."

The words rushed out of Kyra. She had been more frightened than she realized.

"I don't understand," Uliana said.

"Neither do I," Kyra said, and as the words left her mouth, she realized just how little she did understand. Nothing made sense.

Matvei was coming back toward them. "We need to get out of here," he said. "Zed believes the weather won't hold."

Then Matvei peered at Kyra. "You're not covered in ice."

"No, I'm not," she said. "Something strange happened down there."

Matvei frowned at her, as if he didn't want to hear it. He seemed panicked, and, like Alyoshi, Matvei never panicked.

He moved past her and started disassembling the pulley. Uliana hurried to his side.

Kyra packed her equipment quickly, just like she had been trained to do in an emergency. She gathered it up, tucked it under one arm, then walked to the two remaining members of her team. As she passed Alyoshi's harness, she grabbed it too, and dragged it toward the demiglider.

Matvei looked at it, then glanced at Uliana, as if asking her a question.

That simple look—and the only possible question it could be (*do we need to have that weight in the demiglider?*) sent a chill through Kyra.

Her legs were wobbly, but she managed to reach Matvei and Uliana. They were beginning to disassemble the pulley.

"How is he?" Kyra asked.

"Not breathing," Matvei said and walked away.

The words felt like bits of ice, stabbing Kyra. Her gaze met Uliana's. Uliana's expression was carefully blank.

"Where is he?" Kyra asked.

"In the demiglider," Uliana said.

Kyra shook her head, suddenly not sure she had understood Matvei. "Alyoshi will be all right then, right?" Kyra asked. "Once we get him below? Once we find a doctor?"

Uliana shook her head.

Kyra blinked, trying to understand. Maybe she did understand.

"He's ... dead?"

Uliana nodded.

Kyra frowned, feeling unsettled. None of this seemed real. How could he be dead?

And then she remembered the set of his head as he lolled in his harness. Had she waited too long? What if she hadn't taken those few minutes to examine the interior of the cave with the spyglass.

Would Alyoshi have survived?

"I'd like to see him," she said quietly. Maybe then his death would seem real. Surely, she was having these odd thoughts because she didn't believe he was gone.

"He's in the demiglider already," Uliana said. "He's riding back with you."

Kyra almost asked if the others weren't coming back. She was having trouble wrapping her mind around that—which was when she realized she wasn't thinking clearly at all.

Because of the thin air? Because she was just beginning to feel grief? Because this entire trip had been strange and traumatic and not at all what she expected?

What Uliana meant became slowly became clear. Kyra was going to travel back with Alyoshi's corpse in the opposite seat.

Alyoshi's *corpse*.

Kyra pivoted and walked toward the demiglider. There was nothing else to say to the team anyway. She wasn't even sure how she could explain what had happened at the mouth of that cave.

She had never had a climb like that. She wasn't even sure she'd had an experience like that in life in general—where the other person was so clearly having problems, so clearly suffering from something external, and those problems, that external thing, hadn't existed for her at all.

Her stomach was unsettled, her breath uneven, and she was ever so slightly dizzy. She stopped, found the honey water inside her own pack and made herself drink.

The water helped. The honey didn't lift her mood like it usually did, but it cut through her exhaustion. She knew from experience that the energy would not last, but it would at least get her through the next half hour or so.

She put the drink back into her side pack and walked the remaining distance to the demiglider. Zed was on the opposite side, checking the struts on the double wings.

Matvei was loading equipment into the small compartment on the back of the demiglider—and not doing so carefully. He was tossing items in as if they were substitutions for his fists. He clearly wanted to punch something—or someone.

Kyra gave him a wide berth. She approached Zed instead.

His gaze was wary, and maybe filled with warning. She had the sense he didn't want to talk with her either.

"Where is he?" Kyra asked.

Zed swept a hand toward the middle of the demiglider. The bubble to that second section—the section she had ridden in—was open.

"Uliana said he's dead," Kyra said. She'd heard miracle stories about people who looked like they had frozen to death, only to have them thaw and revive.

She knew Zed had heard those stories too, and she respected him enough not to repeat them as if she were questioning what he had just told her.

Zed must have seen all of that on her face. "Take a look for yourself."

She paused, then nodded. She had to use the struts and climb on the wing to get into the demiglider from this angle.

She held the struts gingerly, and put her feet carefully on the supported edges of the wings, like Zed had taught her long ago.

He stopped and watched her, a slight frown on his face. Was he wondering how she managed to move, given she had just completed a difficult climb? Or was he wondering why she was alive and Alyoshi wasn't?

Or both?

She reached the compartment easily. It would have taken very little for her to climb inside, back into her seat.

He was leaning against the far side of the compartment, his legs resting at an unusual angle, one arm at his side and the other trapped beneath him. His head leaned on the edge of the compartment, his hair tangled around his face.

He looked like he was unconscious, not dead.

She climbed in the compartment after all, her movements shaking the demiglider. He didn't move at the disturbance.

She sat beside him and gently touched his arm.

His sleeve was damp, his hair matted. She reached for his face, so she could turn it toward her, just so she could see for herself what was going on.

His skin was like ice. It didn't even really feel like skin. It was too cold and a little rubbery.

It took all of her strength to keep from recoiling. She turned his face toward her.

His eyes were open, which she hadn't expected, and clouded, as if something had covered them, dulling them. His skin was mottled red and white and black. Ice still coated his eyebrows. His lips were chapped and split as if they had been too dry. Something had crusted around his nose—maybe blood, although whatever it was, was awfully dark. The tip of the nose got frostbite first. Maybe that was the blackness she was seeing.

Her heart twisted. Alyoshi was dead. Very clearly, obviously, completely dead.

And he had been covered with ice. He had frostbite and maybe windburn, if the chapping on his cheeks was any indication. He had suffered on that climb, and she had been excited by what she saw, maybe even a tad warm in that strange light.

She had no idea what had happened to him.

Or maybe she should be wondering—what had happened to her?

She slowly released his face. Her fingers left tiny imprints on his skin. She had been grabbing him too tightly.

She took his shoulders, meaning to adjust his position, but his body wasn't moving much at all. It was too early for rigor mortis, wasn't it? Had he been that frozen?

Her stomach flopped, and she was suddenly queasy. She had to look away.

A million excuses ran through her head. She hadn't done this. He had opted to go with her. He had *insisted* on it. But he had wanted to go back before she did, and she had made him wait …

She pushed herself out of that compartment. She couldn't sit there any longer.

She climbed off the side of that demiglider to find herself alone. Zed was helping Matvei and Uliana disassemble the last of the equipment. The clouds had come even closer, and the wind was blowing as strongly as it had on that mountainside—against Alyoshi.

It was getting dark, even though it wasn't quite midday.

All of that had happened in the morning.

Kyra blinked, feeling tears, but they were getting blown about by the wind. She made her way to the others and helped them with the last of the equipment.

The look Matvei gave her was colder than the wind. He gathered more equipment in his arms and walked away from her.

She had seen Matvei grieve a lost companion before. Matvei got angry first, because he didn't want to acknowledge the death.

She didn't blame him. She didn't want to acknowledge Alyoshi's death either.

She took pieces of the pulley and placed them in the bag that the team always carried. Zed took some of the longer pieces of equipment to the demiglider and then, upon arrival, said something to Matvei.

Matvei made a fist, raised it above the demiglider, and Zed caught his hand. Then Matvei shook free and walked away, heading toward the edge of the peak.

Kyra wanted to tell him not to go there, not with the wind coming up, not with the clouds moving in.

But she knew he wouldn't be able to hear her.

Uliana took a bag of equipment to the demiglider, where Zed was repacking what Matvei had placed in the back.

Kyra checked the ground to make sure nothing had fallen. Then she glanced at the sky. The light was almost gone.

She shivered. They had to leave, and soon.

She carried the bag she'd packed to the rear of the demiglider and handed it to Zed. He nodded his receipt, but said nothing. Uliana left and walked toward Matvei.

Kyra hoped Uliana was going to tell him to come to the demiglider.

Kyra waited until Zed was done packing, then she said, "Are we in trouble trying to get down?"

"It's not going to be pretty," he said, "especially with dead weight. I put Alyoshi in the center to balance, but really, he shouldn't be on the demiglider at all."

He said that pointedly as if he expected her to give that order. She couldn't. She *wouldn't*.

"Can we make it down with him on board?" Kyra asked.

"I'm not sure we can make it down, period," Zed said.

Kyra's heart rate increased. "You said going down was easier."

"That day," he said. "That day I took you up, going down would have been easier. But the conditions were different, and this wind …"

He let the sentence trail off. She didn't need to hear the end of it anyway. She knew what he meant.

"Do we have other choices?" she asked.

"I suppose we could camp," he said. "See if things are better tomorrow. But we don't have camping equipment, and there's no real shelter if these clouds turn into the kind of storm I think they will. And if the wind gets any worse, the demiglider might not stay on the peak. We could lose our way down."

"I didn't expect this," she said.

His gaze measured her.

"I hadn't expected it either," he said.

After a minute, he broke the gaze and walked to the front of the demiglider.

Uliana walked to the demiglider, her hand on Matvei's back. His face was red, and he averted his eyes when he saw Kyra. She sighed inwardly, not exactly knowing how to traverse this complete change in her team, in herself, in everything.

She climbed up on the side of the demiglider and crawled into the compartment. She settled, like Zed had taught her the very first time, then put a hand on Alyoshi's damp sleeve.

He didn't notice. Of course, he didn't notice. But she willed him to understand.

"I'm so, so sorry," she whispered. She could say nothing else. She was full of excuses and she needed to set them aside.

She had planned this trip, and he had died on it. He was the first person who had ever died on a trip or something she had planned.

Other professors had lost team members, particularly when the professors were doing dangerous things. That was why no Students or Advanced Students were allowed on dangerous field missions.

There was even discussions about whether Practical Interns should have been allowed along, although she hadn't had any here.

Thank goodness.

Because the uproar would be vast. Alyoshi was well liked.

He was loved—by her too. He'd been a friend forever, and she hadn't listened to him.

Kyra leaned her head back, but kept her arm on his damp sleeve. She didn't want to let him go.

Zed stepped beside her and pushed the bubbleglass down. It clicked into place. He wasn't looking at her either, although his gaze rested on her hand for a moment.

His expression softened, just a little, and then he moved behind her. She didn't turn, but the demiglider shook a little as the bubbleglass covering Uliana and Matvei clicked into place.

They were ready to leave, except for Zed, who had to climb into the cockpit.

As he had done before their launch to the peak of Mount Vitaki, he walked around the demiglider doing other things, things he said Kyra didn't need to know.

The clouds had circled the edge of the peak now dark, almost black. A tiny ray of light pierced through them, and it felt like the light was illuminating her. The light covered her bubbleglass only, and warmed her.

She hadn't realized how cold she had become until that light touched her.

Zed climbed into the cockpit, the demiglider shaking under his weight. He adjusted the dials in front of him. That she did understand because he had explained it to her.

He was opening the wind vents on the windstone tube that ran beneath the demiglider. He needed power to get the demiglider off the mountain top, and more power to let the demiglider plough through those clouds.

Otherwise, with the way the wind was blowing, the demiglider would slam into the mountainside.

Kyra swallowed hard. The demiglider still rocked in the wind. Occasionally a gust would buffet the demiglider, and it would slide just a little.

Zed didn't seem to notice, although his hands worked faster than they had when the demiglider was landing.

His face wasn't showing any tension, but his entire body was.

Then he grabbed the stick with his right hand. With his left, he activated the speaker.

"Brace yourselves," he said. "This is going to be the ride of our lives."

The speaker clinked off. He slammed his left palm on one of the dials and then pulled the stick to the right. The demiglider eased sideways.

Kyra's stomach fluttered as if she was flying.

The demiglider turned all the way around, and she finally understood what Zed was doing.

He was putting the wind behind them—even though they were taking off from the opposite direction they needed to go.

Kyra thought she heard Uliana's voice rise in the back—explaining what was going on to Matvei? Worrying about what Zed was doing? Trying to get Zed's attention?

Kyra didn't know. There was no way to know. She couldn't make out what Uliana was saying. Zed probably hadn't even heard the faint voice.

As the demiglider rocked in the wind, Alyoshi's body slipped a little.

Now, instead of holding it as comfort, or support, or in memory, Kyra was bracing it, just a little.

Maybe she should have grabbed Alyoshi's arm when they were descending, or when they were at the cave's mouth. Would that have changed anything? Would he still be alive?

She shook her head, trying to get those thoughts out of her mind. But it wasn't working, particularly since that ray of golden light still attached itself to her, even as the demiglider moved into different positions.

The floor was vibrating under her feet. Zed had explained that, saying that as the demiglider's windstone tube filled with air, the stored power would make the demiglider seem almost alive.

Of course, with the wind and the encroaching clouds, the movement and the whistle that echoed over the windglass, everything seemed alive at the moment.

Everything except Alyoshi.

The floor's vibration became a shaking, and the shaking nearly rattled her teeth out of her head.

Then, when she thought she couldn't take anymore, the demiglider launched itself forward, wheels on the ground, heading into the clouds.

She felt the lift. There was a difference. No rattling, no vibration, just a sudden smoothness as the demiglider caught some kind of current.

The clouds parted in front of them, unlike when they arrived, but the parting wasn't one-hundred percent. The side of the demiglider with Alyoshi was dark, and rain pelted the windglass, but on her side, the golden sunlight continued as if they were flying under perfect blue skies.

If only she could lean forward, or climb from one compartment to another, so that she could sit by Zed. His compartment was a single-person compartment, and it was half in sunlight and half in rain and clouds.

He didn't seem to notice, though, or if he did, he wasn't letting on. His hands were moving even faster, although a moment ago she would not have thought that possible. He didn't say a word—not that she could hear him—but something in his posture was different.

If she had to guess, she would have thought him panicked. But the Zed she knew didn't panic—about anything.

The demiglider seemed to float upward, but she had no real way of measuring what was happening. The light reflected off her clothing, but Alyoshi was in darkness—except where her hand was touching him.

She peered over her shoulder. The clouds had formed around the back of the demiglider. Only the area where she sat was 100% in the light.

Uliana's cool gaze met hers. Uliana frowned slightly as if to acknowledge she was seeing the changes in the light.

Matvei watched Kyra turn around, but the moment she looked at him, he looked away.

She nodded once, then turned back.

The area in front of the demiglider was covered in clouds.

Zed was flying forward without any visibility at all.

But the demiglider seemed to be moving quicker, and it felt sturdier than it had on the ride here.

He was pushing the stick, and if Kyra squinted, she could see the nose was pointed straight forward.

At some point, he would have to point that nose downward. They were in a valley, but there were a lot of peaks near Mount Vitaki. One wrong turn, and they'd fly right into one.

Kyra took a deep breath and willed this flight to go smoothly. None of them needed more trouble.

As if it heard her thought, the demiglider banked sharply to the right. Zed used both hands to grab the stick, but it seemed to be moving on its own.

Then the demiglider veered upward, and as it did, Kyra saw mountains on her side. If the demiglider hadn't veered, hadn't banked, it would have crashed into them.

Zed had his hands in the air. The stick seemed to be moving on its own.

He glanced over his shoulder at Kyra, his eyes wide—frightened.

Fear gripped her. He wasn't flying the demiglider. He was letting her know that it was out of his control.

She waved a hand at him, as if to say, *Do your job!*

He shrugged and extended his hands even more as if he couldn't do the job at all.

He mimed reaching for the stick, but as he did so, the top seemed to bend away from him, while the middle of the stick didn't bend at all.

Surely that was an illusion of the light. Sticks did not move like that.

The nose of the demiglider turned downward, and the rest of the demiglider followed, going much faster than Kyra would have liked.

Zed wasn't even trying to guide the demiglider. He was hanging onto his seat with both hands. The muscles in his neck stood out as if he was clamping down on his jaw.

Kyra didn't know if Uliana and Matvei could see Zed. Kyra hoped they couldn't, because just looking at him was making her more terrified than she had been on that mountainside before she realized what was going on with Alyoshi.

She wished she could convince herself that what Zed was doing was a normal part of flying the demiglider, but she knew it wasn't. She had asked him on that very first flight why he had the stick, what the dials meant, and why he was there.

Gliders float on air currents, he said. *You have little control of them. But this glider is a* demi*glider for a reason. It needs its pilot. It's too heavy to fly just on air currents. It has a propulsion system. It can and should be steered. It's just not something you hope will make its way down safely.*

She raised her gaze to him now. He was leaning forward as if watching the dials, which had iced over. There was ice in the cockpit? She wasn't cold.

But Alyoshi was. She had just attributed that to the fact that his body was no longer producing any warmth.

If this demiglider goes down, she thought as clearly as if she had spoken the words. *I will die.*

The light expanded suddenly and engulfed the entire demiglider. The clouds receded somewhat, and the ice on the dials melted, leaving beads of water on the front.

Zed reached out cautiously and wiped off the water with his fingers. Then, he grabbed the stick with one hand.

The stick seemed to respond this time.

He visibly let out a breath, then moved the stick. The demiglider continued its downward path.

As the clouds burned off, Kyra realized the demiglider was in the very center of the valley, following the river below. They were off course if they were heading back to the plateau they had taken off from, but there were plenty of places to land near the river.

She let out a breath, finally able to acknowledge just how terrified she had been.

Her fingers were wrapped in the fabric of Alyoshi's sleeve as if she had been leaning on him to give her comfort.

She glanced at him one final time: she had always leaned on him for comfort. Tears threatened for the first time. How had she ignored him? How had she made that mistake? What was *wrong* with her?

She didn't really feel like herself. Was it finally figuring out what was causing the reflection off Mount Vitaki? Or was it that cave? Or was it some kind of reaction to the grief?

She didn't know, and she wasn't quite ready to unpack it yet.

Sunlight covered the entire valley. The flowing brown water of the river gleamed and winked at her as if they both understood some kind of secret.

She twisted in her seat. The horrid dark clouds had taken over the entire top of Mount Vitaki. She couldn't see it at all anymore. And yet, as she looked at it, she wanted to.

Part of her was ready to head back up to the top right now.

And that wasn't like her at all.

She made herself look down, made herself look at the dials.

Zed still clung to the bottom of his seat. The dials still had moisture on the side, and the stick was holding steady, seemingly by itself.

She shuddered just a little. Maybe she was dying. Maybe she had passed out on that trip down the mountainside, and she was hallucinating all of this.

That made as much sense as what she was seeing.

The stick turned, and then the demiglider turned. It continued downward, away from Mount Vitaki.

She unhooked her fingers from Alyoshi's sleeve. Her hand was wet. She wiped it on her pants, feeling just a little ill.

The demiglider was traveling silently. The wind didn't even whistle around it, like it had up above, and the demiglider wasn't moving around like it had. It stayed stable as if whatever propelled it kept it steady too.

Finally, the demiglider settled just above the river. If it went much farther, it would land in the water.

Zed picked up his right hand, squeezed it as if he had hurt it by clinging so hard, and gingerly placed it on the stick. Then he wiped the dials again with his left thumb.

Now, the stick was responding to his touch. He took the demiglider to a new height, moved it slightly away from the river, and slowly turned it around.

Even though she hadn't consulted with him, she knew what he was doing. He was heading back to the plateau they'd launched from, not far from her adobe home, not far from the buildings where she taught students from the Academy how to be archeologists.

The very thought—the word "archeologist"—made her stomach jump with anticipation, and as she acknowledged that, an image of all of those items from the cave rose in her mind.

How had they gotten there? Was there an entrance on the ground that she and her students had missed? That everyone had missed? Should she check for it? Should she send some kind of team to find it all?

She shook herself, trying to rid the thoughts from her head. They were easier to think about than what she would say when the team arrived back at her compound, with Alyoshi dead.

She made herself look outside the demiglider, at the blue sky, and the mountain platform that was just ahead—or seemed to be just ahead. She couldn't really judge distance in this kind of light.

Zed wasn't moving as quickly as he had before, but that hunch in his shoulders, the way he leaned forward … he still seemed panicked to her.

Why wasn't she panicked? Was she numb?

She didn't turn around any longer. Instead, she watched as the ground got closer and closer, and finally, the demiglider bounced along it.

A handful of Practical Interns came out of nearby buildings, smiling and waving, and oh—she didn't want to deal with them.

She should have thought about how to talk to them, about what to do. That was her job, not Uliana's, or Zed's, or Matvei's.

Magnus was with the Practical Interns. Had he brought them to help himself through the long wait?

She wrenched her brain away from that cave, the reflection point, the mountain, and made herself focus on the next few hours.

She had to decide what to do. She had to figure out how to handle this.

And she had to talk to Alyoshi's family.

She didn't have time to contemplate the cave, even though that was all she really wanted to do.

FOUR

Somehow, they got the demiglider unloaded. Somehow, she told everyone—in halting language—that Alyoshi had died up there. The moment went from celebratory to funereal in an instant.

It didn't help that she couldn't explain what had happened—why he froze to death, yet she hadn't been cold at all. She mentioned the cave, the items in it, but no one seemed excited about that. Everyone who listened, except maybe Uliana, seemed surprised that Kyra would talk about the inside of that cave at all.

Kyra had no idea how to thread the emotions. She had no way to know what was normal and what wasn't. Her legs wobbled. She was so tired.

Magnus took her arm and led her to a nearby rock. Then he went back to the Practical Interns and talked with them, gesturing, getting them to unpack the demiglider and deal with Alyoshi's corpse.

Or maybe Magnus had dealt with it.

Kyra didn't watch. She'd worry about all of that a little later. After she sat for a moment and caught her breath.

She found herself looking at Mount Vitaki.

The legends said there was magic on that mountain. The legends said that only a handful of people belonged anywhere near it. The legends said evil could come from that mountain and attack anyone at any time.

She hadn't believed any of it. She wasn't sure she believed the magic part now, but she understood the sense of evil. Whatever had happened to Alyoshi—had been awful, and had seemed personal against him.

The mountain wanted her. It hadn't wanted him at all.

She understood that now. She wished she had understood it while she was on the mountainside, but something had clouded her brain. That desire, which she still felt; that need to get inside that cave, to be near that mountain, to figure out exactly what was going on.

She felt more clearheaded now, but she wasn't sure why.

One thing she *was* sure of: she would be disciplined by Serebro Academy. She might not be able to bring Practical Interns up here again.

She might be called back.

She couldn't be called back.

If the academy demanded that she leave the Razbitay Mountains, she would resign.

Maybe she would resign anyway.

Eventually, the activity settled down. Magnus found his way to her side. He had two mugs of peppermint tea. Of course he had two mugs of peppermint tea.

"There will be a disciplinary hearing," he said quietly, as he handed her a mug. She took it, startled at the warmth.

The steam smelled good. Her stomach growled. She hadn't realized she was hungry. She didn't know how long it had been since she'd eaten.

He sat beside her. She had to scoot over to make room for him on the rock.

"If you go back," he said.

"What?" she asked, before she put the sentences together in her head. *There will be a disciplinary hearing… if you go back.* "Why wouldn't I go back?"

Magnus gave her a sideways smile.

"If you resign and back date it," he said, "you own this discovery, not the academy."

He was being mercenary. At a time like this. She wasn't sure why.

She blinked at him, confused.

"You can't be disciplined then," Magnus said. "And maybe you shouldn't be disciplined anyway. Alyoshi went with you as a friend. He's not part of the archeology department."

Present tense. Part of Magnus was thinking clearly and the other part was not.

"And Uliana and Matvei are locals now," Magnus said. "We'll pay them, you and I. Not the academy."

Kyra frowned at him.

"You found things, right?" Magnus asked. "That's what you said. You found things in that cave."

"Saw things," she said.

A lot of things. Things that didn't belong there in a cave midway up a mountain.

"That might be true," she said. "Why is that important?"

It was important to her, of course. But everything was clouded by Alyoshi's death. The academy would certainly see it that way.

"Because we are at the crossroads of two futures, you and I," Magnus said. "If we go back to Serebro right now, our lives will get picked over. You'll be disciplined and maybe even lose your sinecure. You won't be working with Practical Interns, not after death like this. Your life will never be the same. *Our lives will never be the same.*"

"They won't be anyway," she said.

"That's right," Magnus said. "If we stay, we can control our own future. Maybe even figure out what you discovered."

"You have a hunch," she said.

He nodded. "Remember that legend? The one about the warriors on the mountain?"

She blinked. She had forgotten it, thinking it silly. That warriors had come through a hole in the Razbitay Mountains and nearly destroyed this part of Dorovich. Centuries ago. Maybe even a thousand years ago.

Long before the Qavniatic Protectorate existed. Before anyone wrote things down. Some of the locals liked retailing the legend, but others would shush them as if the legend was unspeakable.

Maybe it was. The legend had the stuff of myth—warriors descending. Half humans, half birds attacking. Creatures never before seen, taking over entire villages.

She had always assumed that was one of the reasons the valley was forbidden—because some thought the mountain dangerous, and others thought the purveyors of this legend crazy.

The danger and the crazy had left centuries ago. The warriors disappeared as if they had never been, and the stories were simply that. Stories to scare children, to keep them away from one of the more dangerous places on the continent.

"What about that legend?" she asked.

"What if the warriors did come out of the mountain?" Magnus asked. "Through that cave. As a surprise."

"There was no way out of that cave," she said, and immediately knew she was wrong. There was. They could have rappelled all the way down to the valley floor from that plateau.

Which begged the question: how had the warriors gotten in the cave in the first place?

Her heart lifted, and as it did, her brain told her she was betraying Alyoshi.

But she wasn't. If she found answers, then maybe she would make his death worthwhile, right? That had been the whole point. To learn what was going on in this little corner of Dorovich.

"Have you done the numbers?" she asked.

Magnus nodded. "I kept getting two sets for today, and they didn't make sense until you returned. Now they do."

She waited. She still hadn't sipped the tea, but the peppermint scent *was* soothing, a thought that made her smile, just a little ruefully.

"If we go back to the academy," he said, "we have a dark future."

"And if we stay?" she asked.

"Then your mission to the mountain truly was auspicious. The Kirilli name will reverberate through the entire history of Dorovich for decades to come."

She had no idea how he knew that. For all she knew, he was making it up. But after the crazy things she had seen today, she was much more willing to believe in his predictions than she had been at any other point in their lives.

Or maybe she just wanted to believe to avoid the discipline that she would face if she left the mountains.

It really wasn't a decision at all.

"All right," she said quietly. "We'll stay."

Magnus hugged her with one arm, pulling her close. Then he let her go, and she felt the loss of him, almost more than she felt the loss of Alyoshi.

"I'll take care of everything," Magnus said. "You just focus on that mountain."

She nodded, then turned slightly on the rock. The sun was setting. A bright white light beamed out of the side of Mount Vitaki and coated her in brilliance.

No one else was touched by the light. No one else even seemed to notice.

It was almost as if the mountain was winking at her, telling her that it too approved of the decision.

She nodded once, in a kind of mental acknowledgment and then turned away.

Even though Magnus said he would handle everything, there were things only she could do. Interactions with the mountain, decisions to be made here in the valley.

She would do all of that.

And she would never go back to Serebro.

Somehow, that thought didn't break her heart.

She wondered now, if anything ever could.

...continued in issue 61.

Copyright © 2022 by Kathryn Kristine Rusch.

Printed in Great Britain
by Amazon